THE TWO CARROT RING

And Other Fascinating Jewelry Stories

JANET METZ WALTER

This book is dedicated to the memory of my mother, Sylvia H. Metz, a loving teacher, who never walked out of the house without makeup and jewelry. As a teacher of young children, she did not have to be decked out in diamonds every day, but she had costume or "fashion" jewelry to match every outfit and she always looked well dressed and professional. It is from her that I developed my own love for jewelry.

It is also dedicated to the memory of my father, Leon Metz who loved to sing and was an incredible dancer. He taught me and my brother, Mike, the love of music, singing, and dancing. But most importantly, through his passion for sports, and for his favorite activity, playing handball, he taught me how to come back from adversity and pursue my own interests.

After both major back surgery and major heart surgery he was told that he would never play handball again, and his answer each time was "Watch me!" and he went back to playing both times.

I was always more interested in reading and writing than sports, and have wanted to be a writer since childhood. I learned to overcome my own obstacles and to pursue my own passions, including writing this book.

CONTENTS

PROLOGUE

*E*very piece of jewelry that someone owns has a story. Some are as simple as

"I inherited this piece from my Grandmother and it is 100 years old."

Others are more involved like *"I sat in the back of a horse drawn carriage while my niece's boyfriend proposed to her in the front."*

Over the years I have found that people enjoy hearing the stories that are attached to pieces of jewelry that they admire on someone. It is a peek into someone's life. I hear lots of stories, from romantic proposals to a request from a customer to make jewelry from the gold fillings extracted from their father's teeth. (We didn't do it. We wound up just buying the gold from them and sending it to be melted.)

In the course of our business, Gold Fire Diamonds, I started a Pinterest board called "Fascinating Jewelry Stories." It is mainly based on stories about pieces of jewelry that have made the news, like the latest Super Bowl Ring, many of which have appeared on our website courtesy of a professional jewelry blogger.

I soon realized that I also have my own jewelry stories that would make an interesting and more personal book for anyone to read.

When I started asking around and proposing the idea to friends and family, I was amazed at the response. Everyone had at least one story, and everyone wanted to tell it. People even recommended friends who said that they had stories to tell me.

And so the book was born. Some of the stories are simple, but the jewelry piece is pretty or unusual. Some are more dramatic, and I decided to include all of the stories because every story has meaning to the person who shared it, and although some are similar, each has a slightly different twist.

Jewelry goes in and out of style but it is my belief that if you have a piece, or several, that mean something very special to you, there is no reason not to wear it, no matter how old or "dated" it is.

If you have a few pieces that you really no longer wear that are just hanging out in a box or drawer, redesign it into something that you would be happy to wear. We can help you with that. There is a whole chapter in the book about repurposed jewelry.

So here is the first edition. If you have stories and would like to see your story in print for another edition, contact me through my email info@goldfirediamonds.com and I will tell you how to submit your story.

Meanwhile delve into the personal stories of the people who made this book possible.

Janet Metz Walter

Chapter One

PROPOSALS

Some are simple, some are planned out for weeks. You think of it as a guy going down on one knee and giving the girl the ring. And what about the ring?
Here are four stories that talk about rings and proposals. Not exactly what you might expect!

THE STONE SWITCH

When I turned eighteen I decided that I wanted to travel and see the world. I stayed in Israel for a while, and I actually traveled extensively for eight years until I was twenty-five.

When I was finally back home for a while and had a job teaching, I was set up on a blind date with Marty. That night after the date I came home and told my family that I had met the guy I was going to marry.

One month later, he took me to a family party. It was the first time he had taken a girl to meet his family, and the family knew that I was the one.

He was planning to propose to me on my birthday in June, but about two months before that he started casually talking about having children and a few other things and I asked him if that meant that he was planning to marry me, so he said yes and proposed.

Marty is not a jewelry person and he wasn't planning the proposal the way it went, so I did not get an engagement ring. We were planning to get married in September so we decided to go together to a jeweler that was recommended to us to pick out a ring. I wanted an opal.

There are several different kinds of opals. The most common one is a blue or turquoise color that has other colors in it. I wanted the fiery one that gives off flashes of bright colors.

I picked out a stone that I liked and then picked out a setting. When we went back to the jeweler to pick up the ring, it was very obvious that he had switched the stone. It was white. We refused to take the ring and that was the end of it. I really did not care if I had the ring, as long as I had the man that I loved.

The jeweler had been recommended to us, but he turned out not to be very honest. It is always important if you are having something made to order to make sure that you go to a reliable honest jeweler who will give you what you are asking for and not try to make you pay for something you did not choose.

Meanwhile, I got only one other jewelry gift in my life, but several years ago I took a course in making beaded jewelry and I have turned it into a hobby. I make it for friends and relatives and sell some of it at craft fairs and holiday boutiques. Now I have as much jewelry as I want, any time I want it.

Contributed by Marla S

HOW TO SAFELY BUY A HUSBAND

It was a rainy summer evening as I walked up 47th Street toward the Jewelers and Dealers Exchange in Manhattan. I was bringing back the birthday present I had bought for myself—a dainty gold bracelet-watch with small diamonds all around the face. Not because I didn't like it but because my friend had been shocked when I showed her my splurge: "It doesn't have a safety chain! What if the lock opens? You'll lose the watch!"

"She's right!" I thought, so I decided to get it done right away.

Pushing the heavy glass doors open as I closed my umbrella, I headed down the center aisle to L. Tropin Jewelers where I expected to find Dave, the guy who had sold me the watch. But Dave wasn't there. Another man was behind the counter talking animatedly to a couple standing in front of him. When he saw me standing there, he smiled at me and motioned to a stool. "Please have a seat. I'll be with you soon."

About two minutes later the couple left and Larry, the L in L. Tropin, gave me a broad grin and asked how he could help me. "I was here on Friday and bought this watch from Dave. My friend suggested I put a safety chain on it, just in case."

"Oh, Dave's my brother-in-law. No problem!" he said. "Let me take care of that for you right now. Don't go away!" And he sped off down the aisle and up the stairs. He was back in a heartbeat and began to make small talk. "I'll have that for you in a few minutes."

"Wow! What great service," I thought to myself.

So we began to talk. One thing led to another, and he asked me for a date. Looking at him I thought to myself, "He's an older guy and probably married." So I said to him, "I don't date married guys!"

"I'm not married," he protested. "Really! Would you like to go to a horse show on Long Island on Sunday? I could pick you up at 10 AM and we'd spend the day out east. I promise I'll get you home before dark!"

There was such a sweet pleading in his blue eyes, and I figured how dangerous can a man with a jewelry business be? Plus, going to a horse show sounded exotic. So I said yes.

Sunday morning at 10 AM he arrived at my doorstep (probably the only time in the 42 years we would be together that he was on time!) and whisked me off to Stony Brook for the horse show. As we drove the 40+ miles in his green Corvette with the top down, we laughed and chatted. We discovered we both loved to dance, loved animals of every sort, and enjoyed eating at all kinds of restaurants.

Before we arrived in Stony Brook, we had a date for dinner the next evening; and eleven months later we were married.

I sometimes wonder what my life would have been like if I hadn't brought that watch back for a safety chain! Would I have had the long, exciting and safe marriage that I so fortunately had?

Contributed by MarciaGrace

FOUR DIAMONDS

*D*uring WWII my husband Shelly's father had a business selling sewing notions.

As his business became more successful, he decided to invest in some diamonds.

He purchased four diamonds, one for his wife and one for each of his three young sons to be put away and eventually used for engagement rings.

He bought three round diamonds and one emerald cut, which is rectangular in shape.

People who are not that knowledgeable about diamonds may not realize that diamond shapes actually go in and out of style. Round diamonds are the most classic and have remained popular throughout the decades. In the forties when his father made the purchase, both round and emerald cut were in fashion.

Emerald cut diamonds remained popular in the fifties; but when Ascher cut diamonds that are more square in shape became stylish in the sixties, emerald cuts became a little outdated.

The boys were very young when the diamonds were purchased, so his mom made a necklace for herself out of one of the round diamonds and a ring out of the emerald cut.

In the mid 1950's the first son got engaged and got one of the round diamonds, followed a few years later by the second son who got the second round diamond.

Their father was happy to see them using the stones that he had been saving for them.

Unfortunately in 1966 when Shelly was in his last year of college, his father passed away.

I met Shelly in November of 1969. He lived in Queens and I came from Long Island. We met at a singles dance on Long Island and became engaged six weeks later in January of 1970. We were married the following July.

When he asked for my hand in marriage, he didn't have far to go for the ring. His mother had the third stone, the emerald cut diamond, all ready for him and even mounted in a ring. You would think that she would have given the third round stone to her third son, but she liked her necklace and decided to give him the emerald cut ring. It was a little dated by that time; but since she had kept the other round stone for herself, that's what she had to give Shelly.

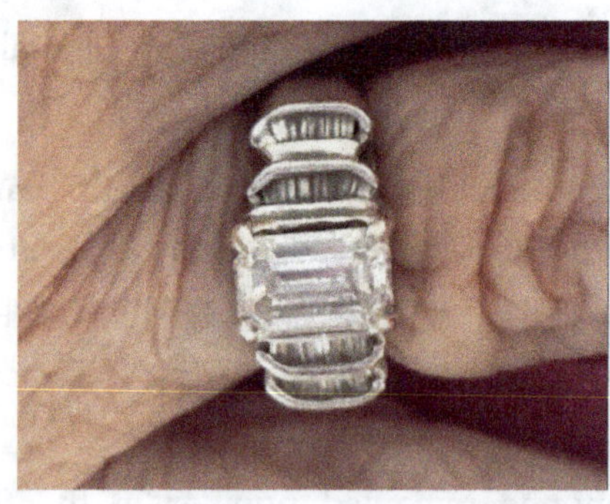

I loved it. It is now in its third setting, but it is still my engagement ring, and I am still wearing it. Funny to say but it has come back into style 49 years later. I don't care if it's in style or not. It is my ring.

I always say "I got the last, but I got the best!"

Contributed by Lani

My niece Debbie's boyfriend, Sam, called me up one day and told me he planned on proposing to Debbie and wanted to pick out a ring.

I went through all the steps of helping him do that. First, we established a price range that he wanted to spend. I needed to know the size of the stone he was thinking of, the shape and the quality. I showed him a few stones and he picked the one he liked.

Then we picked out a setting. He gave me an idea of what he had in mind, and we looked at pictures.

He had to let me know her ring size.

I had the ring made for him, and we arranged to meet in Manhattan for him to pick it up.

He suggested that I meet him for dinner with my daughter Donna who lives in the city, and he told me that he asked Debbie to come to dinner also.

We didn't quite know what his plan was; but before Debbie arrived, he said that he planned on proposing that very evening. He was going to take a horse-drawn carriage ride through Central Park and propose in the carriage.

We thought that that was very romantic except for the fact that it was about 25 degrees outside, a little chilly for a carriage ride; but he said he didn't care, this was his plan.

We had a lovely dinner and started to say goodbye when Sam told us and Debbie that he wanted to go for a carriage ride and he wanted us to come with them.

I took him aside and told him that we did not belong in the carriage when he was proposing to Debbie. He insisted that we were family and he wanted us there to witness the happy moment.

He found a carriage and told us to climb in the back while he and Debbie climbed in the front. We were freezing and felt a little awkward about the situation. Fortunately, there was a blanket in the carriage. Even Debbie couldn't quite understand this harebrained idea until Sam took out the ring and proposed to her in the front of the carriage with me and Donna sitting there in the back. She was surprised and happy and, of course, she said "yes."

It was romantic and funny at the same time.

The ride ended and then we finally parted company, wishing them congratulations and a future of happiness as we all went home to warm up.

While I often deliver engagement rings to prospective grooms, this was the first time I got to see the actual proposal! Quite an interesting experience.

Contributed by Ken Walter

Chapter Two

GIFTS

Gifts aren't always for an occasion. Especially jewelry gifts. They come to you for a lot of different reasons. These are the ones that will make you smile, and bring you into people's lives.

THE TWO CARROT RING AND THE CENTRAL PARK CHARM

When my father George and his twin brother came home from the service after WWII, they moved back in with their widowed father. He gave them both jobs in his advertising and display business.

My father was actually very artistic and talented, and he learned the business well. As the business expanded, they found a need for a bookkeeper; and they hired a lady named Phyllis who applied for the job.

My father was very personable with a great sense of humor, and he flirted with all the women in the company. Employees were forbidden to date each other, but my grandfather thought that Phyllis might be nice for my father's brother who was much quieter and more subdued than my father, so they went out on a couple of dates. But Phyllis was more interested in George, the brother who always made her laugh.

When she told her mother how charming and funny George was, her mother was not happy. "You need this job," she told her daughter. "You cannot risk getting fired by dating the boss's son when it is forbidden."

But Phyllis really liked the boss's son; and he was really getting to like her, too. They were very comfortable together and developed a very nice relationship. So Phyllis had to be very careful about how she interacted with George at work; but they found ways to be together, both during working hours and after work.

They said they weren't really dates because he never spent money on her. His father didn't pay him a very good salary even though he was a very good worker; but since he was living at home and not paying room and board, his father did not see the need to pay him a lot of money. But George was very resourceful. He found lots of free places to take Phyllis.

They would go to free museums and browse the exhibits at the art museums, paintings, and sculptures by famous artists. At The Museum of Natural History, there were dinosaurs whose bones stretched from one end of a room to the other and fascinating colorful exhibits of natural gemstones and ones that were set into the jewelry of royalty.

They would walk up and down Fifth Avenue at Christmas time to see the lights and look at the decorated windows in the big department stores.

The nicest time, however, was lunchtime. The office was close to Central Park and their favorite thing to do on a nice day was to sit on a bench in the park and share a sandwich. They would talk or watch birds or people watch. They had a favorite bench in the park that they would always sit on. It always seemed to be waiting for them.

As time passed George realized that he was in love with Phyllis as she was with him. He was ready to propose.

Diamonds are measured in carat weight. For jewelry, they are cut into sizes from tiny stones that could weigh 1/10 of a carat to huge stones that could weigh ten carats or more. Most engagement rings at the time averaged anywhere from ¼ of a carat to 2 carats. But George couldn't really afford a nice ring.

At the time Woolworth's sold silly "two carrot" rings that were actually two little plastic carrots. So after 10 months, George bought Phyllis a two carrot ring from Woolworth's and proposed.

They were married in 1949. My father went on to start his own advertising and display business and they started a family.

About five years later, he was doing well and decided to design a gift for my mother. He had a lot of friends in the jewelry industry on 47th Street. He designed a gold charm that depicted their bench in Central Park with the lamp post, the birds and even the street sign. He took the drawing to one of his jeweler friends who made up the charm for him.

The charm had a big circle of gold around it but it was too big for my mother to wear around her neck so she had the large gold circle removed. A few years later my father designed a bracelet for her to hang the charm from. Charm bracelets were very popular at that time.

Eventually, they moved to Long Island to raise their family. They enjoyed a happy life. There would be other presents of jewelry but nothing as special as that charm.

On my mother and father's 50th wedding anniversary in 1999, my father arranged for them to stay in the Plaza Hotel near Central Park and to go into the park in the afternoon and sit on their bench which had been changed, but it was fine. It was a beautiful Anniversary. They were always perfect for each other.

By the way, the back of the charm is inscribed "This is our life, 7/48 till forever." That's when they first dated, July 1948.

The painting on the first page and the poem were done by my mother about their special bench in Central Park.

Contributed by D. Sabel

THIS IS WHERE

This is where I fell in love,
With a summer moon high up above.
But oh that was so long ago,
Sixty plus years or so.

As we sat in Central Park,
The sun went down, it was almost dark.
He stole a kiss, just one that night.
That was the start of a love so right.

Life is not simple, there's always a wrinkle.
He was my boss's son, this boy with a twinkle.
I'd be fired for sure, if his father should know,
And the job came first, before any beau.

But he broke down my defenses with one more kiss,
And then another, I couldn't resist.
He hadn't a job, he didn't have any money,
So we'd meet at the bench, whether rainy or sunny.

That was so very long ago,
And we were so in love.
We married a few months later,
With blessings from above.

The years went by, they truly flew.
Soon it was fifty and we knew what we'd do.
We went to sit in the park once more,
Just as we had done before.

They changed the bench,
The one we claimed, but it didn't matter now.
It was there when we first fell in love,
And "this is where" somehow.

CHARM BRACELET

uthor's Note:

In the 1950s and '60s one of the most popular gifts for a Sweet 16 or
other special occasion was a charm bracelet. It consisted of a gold link

chain with one or two charms to denote the occasion—such as a calendar with the date, possibly a religious charm, an initial, or a charm to denote a favorite sport or hobby.

The charms were attached to the bracelet by the jeweler, and a charm was added for each special occasion to follow, such as graduation from high school, then college, engagement, etc. Many of the charms were engraved by the jeweler with a date or the name of the school.

A more mature woman might get charms for her marriage and each of her children.

People would look at the charms and comment on the occasion. Eventually, the bracelet would get a little heavy, cumbersome and noisy and women would tuck them away as a remembrance and move on to simpler jewelry.

In 2000 a company called Pandora, founded by a Danish couple in 1982, introduced the Pandora charm bracelet that consisted of beadlike charms rather than heavy, dangling charms. The charms are not personalized, but there are hundreds of charms to choose from to personalize the bracelet. The company quickly gained worldwide acclaim.

MY BIRTHDAY GIFT

For my 65th birthday, my children gave me a birthday party. They decided to give me a Pandora bracelet. In addition to the bracelet, each of my children decided to give me a charm to go on the bracelet. The idea blossomed as my husband decided to give me a charm, as well as my children's spouses, my sister and my two nieces.

At my party, I was first given the empty bracelet and then each person or persons who were giving me a charm brought it up and explained in front of everyone their reason for choosing that particular charm for me.

They also gave me a full box of tissues!

I wear this piece just about every day and I am often asked about how I chose the charms. I just smile and say there is a story behind each charm.

In case you are wondering, there are 22 charms on this bracelet, and each one of them is as special as the others.

Contributed by Lanie

My mother started her business in the basement of our house on Long Island. She sold clothing, jewelry, and accessories.

Eventually, enough people in the neighborhood and surrounding towns got to know her; and she moved her business to a shop in town until my parents decided to move to Florida.

When she moved to Florida, my mom got a job with Mayors, a well known jewelry store.

It was perfect for her. My mom was a stylish woman whose hair had turned silvery grey at a very early age. In the '80s when big hair was in style my mom always stood out in a crowd.

Her job made it easy for her to give me gifts of jewelry. The problem was that her taste was not my taste. I preferred artistic crafty jewelry and did not care so much about expensive fashion jewelry. But how could I tell my mother that I did not like a beautiful gift she gave me?

So I accepted the jewelry and wore it occasionally. We lived in different parts of the country and she had no way of knowing how much I did or did not wear the jewelry. Once I lost a gold hoop earring and she sent me a single matching hoop. She must have bought another set and just kept the other earring.

She sent me a Cartier watch and an amethyst ring, as well as other jewelry, over a period of time. I actually did pick out the watch and she got it for me at a very discounted price so that I wear it every day.

When my mom passed away, I realized that the possessions I had left of her were the pieces of jewelry that she had given me over the years; and now I cherish them as I think about her and cherish her memory.

Contributed by Amy Haft

INSPIRATION NECKLACE

I worked at Kennedy Space Center. Having two engineering degrees—mechanical and nuclear engineering—I was the assistant spacecraft test manager and was employed by Grumman. That's why I ultimately landed on Long Island.

I met many astronauts and am very proud of our accomplishments during that period. There was a piece published in the *Long Island Business Review* commemorating 50 years of the Lunar Module this year. I did an interview. You might find it interesting.

My work and background inspired me to design this necklace. We give it to all the women/girls in our family. We started this tradition in 1987. At that time we had three daughters. Today we have two additional daughters-in-law and 10 granddaughters. Each necklace includes a handwritten message:

"All of my daughters, daughters-in-law, and granddaughters were given this gift. It symbolizes the thought... women control the earth. I've had these symbols made for those closest to me. Wear it throughout your life. The future is yours, it's in your hands".

We had the necklaces made by a friend. It contains some sort of crystal...it's so long ago.

I think the concept of the necklace was my belief that women have all the power in their hands but need to believe inside that they can do anything they want. I love to watch my daughters hold on to it when they are wearing it. I believe and I hope it is there to remind and reinforce their decision making. It's the tangible object reinforcing their actions.

"Never tell me the sky is the limit when I helped put footprints on the moon!"

Contributed by Joseph W. Tucciarone

I love jewelry and I owned a lot of it. I was always decked out in necklaces, rings, and bracelets; and I am sure there were people who noticed my jewelry.

I had gone through a difficult divorce 6 months before the incident and I moved into a three-story walk-up apartment on the top floor of a building in Florida.

I had no idea that I really wasn't safe, but there was some kind of attic above my apartment; and apparently, there was someone who had been watching me and knew when I would be out of the apartment for a period of time.

I was there a week when someone who obviously was familiar with the layout of the building cut a hole from the attic into my apartment when they knew I wasn't there.

It must have been planned because the thieves made off with most of my furniture and 23 pieces of jewelry, some of which had been gifts. I was totally devastated.

My mom was also devastated for me. I had just been through such a difficult time, I was getting my life together and now this.

She had a hamsa which is an amulet or charm in the shape of a human hand, popular throughout the Middle East and North Africa. It is used in jewelry and wall hangings and is recognized by all religions as a symbol of blessings, power, and strength. It is also considered to deflect the evil eye and many of them have an eye symbol as part of their design. It is considered to be good luck.

My mother always wore it. It did not have an eye but it did have a diamond in it.

Without even thinking twice, she decided to give it to me to help me get through the mind-blowing sadness of losing everything, from my marriage to my possessions.

I have never taken it off even when I had to have major surgery. I convinced the doctors not to remove it. It is a symbol of my mother's unconditional love for me.

It must be good luck because it got me through the surgery and terrible illness, and I am now fully recovered and living a beautiful life surrounded by family and friends.

Contributed by Steve Bauer

A WEDDING GIFT AND AN ANNIVERSARY GIFT

$\mathcal{M}$y fiancé and I started living together a few months before our wedding.

My mother had passed away when I was young and I was planning to wear her pearl necklace on my wedding day.

One day shortly before my wedding I was walking into our apartment. The door was slightly ajar. As I got into the apartment I saw something hanging from the doorknob. It was a bracelet made of two strands of pearls.

As a surprise wedding gift, my fiancé had taken my mother's necklace to a jeweler and had the pearls matched for size and color and had this beautiful bracelet made for me to wear along with the necklace. He explained that the necklace was "something old" and this was "something new."

My fiancé would not have struck anyone as a sentimental guy. He was a little tough and drove a motorcycle, but inside he was very loving and thoughtful and I was very touched by this beautiful gift.

MOST UNUSUAL STONE

My husband wanted to get me a special piece of jewelry for my 20th anniversary.

I thought about it and decided that I wanted a star sapphire ring.

A star sapphire is a solid stone, most common in blue, but it also comes in other colors. In the middle of the stone is a white "star" that radiates rays from the center of the stone outward. It changes with the light as you move it.

We started shopping for rings that we liked. We went to several stores and some had interesting pieces of jewelry. In one store we found a beautiful and unusual stone called a Chalcedony. It was not a star sapphire but resembles a moonstone. It was a solid medium blue. We were told that it was very expensive and mostly sold in very high end stores.

I fell in love with it and we bought it.

We then found a picture of a setting that we liked. We showed the picture to our friend who is a jeweler and he designed it and made up the ring for me.

We both loved it so much that my husband decided to buy me

matching earrings. I was thrilled. I did not know anyone who had jewelry containing this stone and it became very special to me.

One day I was shopping and someone spotted my ring. She was wearing a ring with the same stone and told me she had indeed found it in a very high end store.

I actually found out later that the stone could be found on some websites that sold unusual jewelry but I still know that very few people including jewelers are not familiar with the stone and I still consider it a very special gift.

Contributed by Judy S

I was born in and married in Bulgaria; and when my older daughter was 8, we decided to travel the world with the intention of settling in Israel. Instead, we wound up in Japan because, as a scientist, my husband would have had difficulty finding a job in Israel due to a great influx of Russian scientists there. We spent two years in Japan: the first year strange as we got used to the different culture and the second year beautiful. After two years we left Japan and established a home in the US.

At the time of this story, my older daughter was 15. There was never an opportune time for a second child, yet I always wanted to have 10 children. Obviously, at age 35 this was not meant to be; and I told my husband I would be really unhappy if we remained with just one child. Unfortunately, since it wasn't happening naturally, we went to a fertility specialist. We tried artificial insemination, and we were anxiously awaiting the results when my dear friend invited us to her birthday party.

We'd been through a lot together—raised our children together and struggled together in our home country—and I wanted to give my friend a memorable gift for her birthday. I went to Macy's and purchased a ring made of white and yellow gold topped with three little diamonds. I can't explain why, but I was immediately attracted to the ring. It wasn't showy, it was just simply and understatedly elegant. Plus, the combination of both white and yellow gold solved so many problems as you can wear both silver and gold-colored jewelry with it. I thought this would be a very practical gift for my friend and she would love it!

A few days later, I discovered I was pregnant! Excited about it is mildly put. I was over the moon! Somehow I thought about this ring—it will forever remind me of the time I learned I was pregnant for the second time. I thought I should keep it and buy my friend another present, so that is what I did.

Later, as my pregnancy advanced, all hell broke loose. Suffice it to say I got really sick. We weren't sure if the baby would survive; but thankfully, she did, although she was born very premature. We named her Peri.

Peri had some delays in the beginning, and I was always anxious for her to reach her developmental milestones. Now she is a strong, super-intelligent, beautiful girl, a politically engaged feminist, who coincidentally turned 16 exactly as I am writing this story.

I wear the ring often, although I own a lot of more beautiful pieces—some antiques with their own stories. However, this ring is my reminder of the pure joy I felt in learning I was pregnant.

We call it the Peri ring.

Contributed by Liza Micheva

MY MARRIAGE GIFT & THE BLUE AND WHITE RING

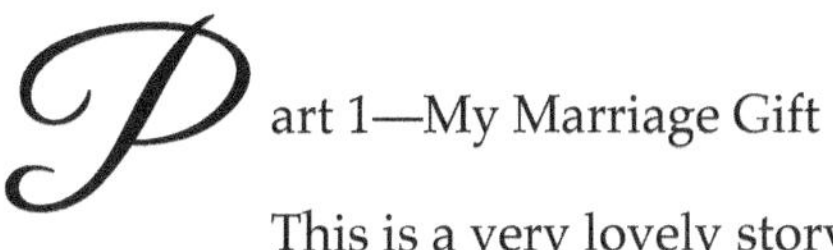art 1—My Marriage Gift

This is a very lovely story.

When I met my husband Steve, he told me that his mother passed away when he was fifteen. It was a very sad and difficult time for him. While we were dating and falling in love, he told me little things about her and his family. Eventually, his father remarried and I was happy to finally meet him and his new wife.

Shortly before our wedding, my future father-in-law came down to Long Island from Rochester, NY. He had with him a beautiful diamond cocktail ring set in platinum that had belonged to his wife. It had been designed by her brother-in-law who was a jeweler in Manhattan and had handpicked the diamonds especially for her.

He had held on to it for seventeen years. That evening, without even telling his son what he planned to do, he handed the ring to me and told me that he wanted me to have it. I was very touched by the gesture and by my future father-in-law's acceptance of me as his future daughter-in-law.

I love the ring and wear it often. I have told my daughter that one day the ring will be passed down to her, but she had to promise that she can never change it or reset it because it was specially designed for her grandmother.

Part 2—The Blue and White Ring

I bought a ring in Aruba many years ago. It's very unusual, with blue and white diamonds in the shape of little florets. I loved it and decided to alternate it on my right hand with my mother-in-law's cocktail ring.

I keep my smaller pieces of jewelry in a little pouch. One day I took off the blue and white ring to switch it with the cocktail ring and put it back in the pouch, or so I thought. Several weeks later when I decided to put the blue and white ring back on, I was stunned to realize that it wasn't in the pouch! It was missing!

Did I unthinkingly put it someplace else? I looked everywhere—in drawers, on the floor, under the bed, and in my jewelry box—all to no avail. Needless to say, I was heartbroken to lose the beautiful ring that I loved, but I had to accept the fact that it was gone.

Several years later we decided to replace our mattress and box spring, and we moved the old set aside for the delivery men to take away. My husband decided to vacuum before the new bedding arrived. He was being extremely thorough and moved the bed frame to vacuum around it. There, under the wheel of the bed frame, laying flat in the indentation made by the wheel which it probably fell into when the frame was moved, was the blue and white ring. It was in perfect condition!

The beautiful ring that I had missed so much had come back to me, and I slept on my new mattress that night a very happy person.

Contributed by Gail Grossman

WHAT REALLY IS ART DECO JEWELRY?

Art Deco is the shortened name of a style of art and architecture that became popular at an exhibit at the World's Fair in Paris in 1925. Authentic jewelry from this period was made between 1920 and 1935. The jewelry featured European cut diamonds rather than modern round brilliant diamonds.

Art Deco featured geometric designs in both jewelry and architecture. The jewelry was fit for the roaring '20s flapper era with earrings and beautiful filigree rings, bracelets and pendants made primarily out of platinum or white gold. Many contained colored stones and most pieces featured symmetrical designs whether or not they were geometric.

The filigree designs were extensively detailed, and most often the stones were specifically cut to fit the design. They were individually crafted, not made out of wax molds. Even if the pieces were similar, like snowflakes, no two were exactly alike.

Of course, there have been many imitations over the years. A genuine Art Deco piece is not made out of 14K gold and was only made during that time period.

I was lucky enough to have been gifted with my mother-in-law Laura Walter's two Art Deco rings when she decided to no longer wear them. One of them has a ring guard on it and fits perfectly on my right ring finger. I wear it for dressy occasions. The other one fits perfectly on my pointer finger and I wear it several times a week as a complement to whatever other white gold or silver rings I am wearing at the time. It is difficult to see but it contains four triangular sapphires.

I always have to smile when someone stops me and marvels at the ring, telling me that they have a similar ring that they inherited from their mother or grandmother. And everyone says they love it!

Contributed by Janet Metz Walter

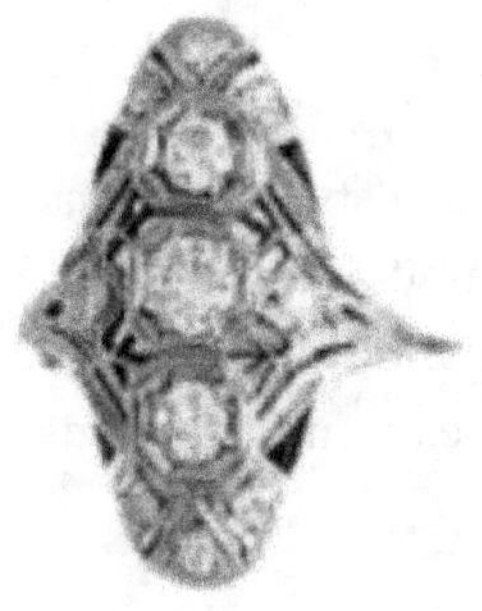 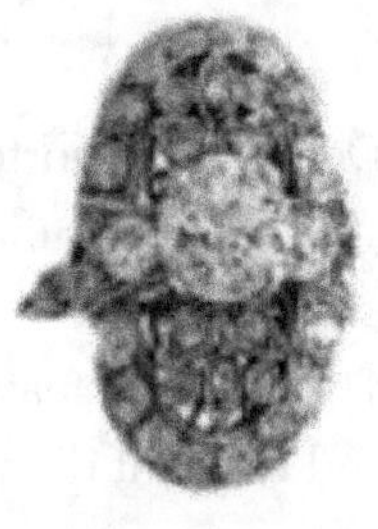

GIFT FROM GRANDMA

When I was 19 I was a student nurse in New York. During that summer, I took a trip to Israel to visit my sister and her family who were living there. I spent the summer volunteering at Hadassah Hospital.

While in Jerusalem, I picked out a gift to bring home to my mother. It was a Jewish star that she wore regularly. As she got older she had difficulty fastening it, so she took it to a jeweler who fashioned a magnetic clasp for her.

When my mom passed away two and a half years ago, the family distributed her jewelry. We wanted each of the grandchildren to have something to remember her. My granddaughter fell in love with her great grandmother's star. She was fourteen.

We gave it to her as a gift from her great grandmother, with a picture of my mother wearing the star. She now wears it all the time and has not taken it off.

Contributed by Dona M

More than a smile, these stories will bring on a giggle.

THE RING IN THE LADIES' ROOM

*A*bout 15 years ago my friend Wendy and I and our husbands were attending the wedding of our friend Ellen's daughter, Beth.

There is an old joke that women who are together in public always go to the bathroom in pairs. Well, the reason for this is that they find an opportune time when there is a break in the music, or their order was taken and they are waiting for their food and they take advantage of the downtime. When a break came in the music, Wendy and I decided to go to the bathroom—together.

The people in the bathroom were finishing up at the sinks. What do we do at the sinks? Wash our hands, comb our hair, put on lipstick, chat a bit. It isn't a secret ritual.

It happened that there were two open stalls next to each other and Wendy and I each went into one. This was a typical public Ladies Room where there was a metal box attached to the wall that held two rolls of toilet paper and had a flat top.

As I locked the door of my stall, Wendy called to me from the other stall saying, "You won't believe this. There is a big diamond ring sitting on top of the toilet paper box."

"Who on earth would take off their diamond ring in a public bathroom and leave it on top of the toilet paper box?" I asked, obviously a rhetorical question.

"Who knows?" Wendy replied. "But I guess I will take it and give it to Ellen and let her figure out who it belongs to."

Just then, an obviously elderly woman from the sound of her voice came into the bathroom, knocked on Wendy's stall and yelled, "Is anybody in there?"

"No," I'm thinking. "Someone locked the door from inside and crawled out from underneath."

"Yes, there's someone in here," Wendy replied.

"Do you see a ring in there?"

Wendy decided to rattle her cage a bit. "What kind of ring?" Wendy asked.

"A diamond ring," she replied a little nervously.

"Describe it," Wendy pursued, still from behind the closed door.

By this time, I was finished and had to see who this character was. It was indeed an elderly woman who Ellen later told me was her mother's sister.

The woman described the ring, and Wendy came out of the stall with the ring in her hand. The woman thanked Wendy profusely, and Wendy told her that she was lucky that she was honest enough to return the ring, as someone else could have easily stolen it. Now, she had to ask the question of the minute—"Why on earth would you take off a diamond ring in a public bathroom and lay it down on top of the toilet paper box?"

Wendy and I looked at each other in amazement as the woman

explained, "I didn't want the ring to rip my pantyhose when I was pulling it up."

When she left the bathroom, I did a scale with my hands. "Let's see now," (as I moved my right hand down and my left hand up). $2.99 pantyhose versus (I moved my right hand up and my left hand down) $5,000 ring. Brilliant decision."

We still laugh about it to this day.

Contributed by Janet Metz Walter

THE JEWELRY IN THE COMMODE

When my mom Anne entered hospice in Feb 2012, she whispered to me that she had jewelry in a plastic baggie in the toilet.

Now, my mom did not have jewels per se but loved unique, handmade silver pieces and only had a few. No diamonds, rubies or gold jewelry, just her wedding ring.

I went to her apartment and, of course, looked in the toilet, thinking that she had somehow attached the baggie to it. Nope. Nothing. I looked in the toilet tank and didn't see anything.

It then occurred to me that maybe she meant the portable commode in the bedroom at hospice that she had never, ever used. She had put a pretty cover over the seat lid and piled all the books she was reading on top of it.

When I cleared off the top, sure enough, there was a small baggie attached to the "chamber pot." In the baggie were two or three silver rings, a handmade bracelet, and silver earrings. These were all sentimental pieces since my dad had given them to her over the years.

As you can imagine, they are among my most sentimental and prized possessions from my mom. A funny aside is that my daughter will only wear silver jewelry and has worn the bracelet since my mom passed.

Someday she will get the rest of the pieces.

Contributed by Betty Jo Lehrman Chin

SEEING DOUBLE

*A*bout 20 years ago for a birthday or anniversary, my husband came home with a blue Tiffany box. I opened it up to find one of those beautiful floating Tiffany diamonds on a platinum chain. I wore it all the time.

A year later for the same occasion, he again came home with a Tiffany box. I assumed he went back because he knew how much I loved the other necklace. Well, I opened it up and to my surprise, I found the exact same necklace in the box. He bought me the exact same one. He refused to believe I already had it. I had to go get my jewelry box and hold it up to the new one so he could see it.

We still laugh about that expensive error today.

Fortunately, Tiffany was fine with the return. And I recently recast the original into a more updated setting that I love. So it remains one of my favorite pieces.

Contributed by Ellen W

GINGER

There is a commercial on TV now, where a dog keeps bringing home odd things like a woman's bra and a plunger. I guess it is pretty common.

When I was still living at home, my parents decided to get a dog. They got a beautiful Golden Retriever and named her Ginger.

My parents live on a large wooded property, and Ginger was mostly an outside dog. There were neighbors in the vicinity, and Ginger spent her days trolling the woods and the neighbors' backyards for things to bring home. Every week she brought home a large French bread baguette. It took months to figure out that a neighbor we hardly knew was giving it to her and she scarfed it up in a couple of bites but not till she brought it home to show us.

She used to go to a local creek for a dip in the summer and then come home with various surprises —hats, cups, even baby chicks. And yes she did bring home a bra. The biggest bra I have ever seen! She would come running through the woods with whatever her catch of the day was and leave it at her water bowl in the mudroom by the garage.

One day she came home with a little purse. When I looked inside, I found a 14K gold butterfly necklace. It was beautiful! I couldn't keep it, knowing someone else lost it. We took it to the police station and told them the story. They laughed and said they would try to find the owner. We never heard from them again. I'm not sure if the owner was ever reunited with her necklace or if the wife or girlfriend of one of the cops got a pretty present.

If Ginger could talk, we would have asked her where she found it and returned it to the owner.

Contributed by Debra Young

Chapter Four

INHERITANCE

The most common way of acquiring jewelry. Some of it brings happy memories, some of it will bring a tear. Sometimes you will love the jewelry you inherit, sometimes you won't. Travel back in time to read the stories of life long ago that became life today.

THE RINGS IN THE VAULT

When my brother was getting married, my mother decided to reset her engagement ring for the wedding. My husband Ken had recently gotten a job for a jewelry manufacturer, and she asked him to help her with her ring.

He brought home books and told her to look them over and choose a style she liked. At that time rings with matching wedding band jackets or inserts were very popular.

My mother picked out a beautiful set. There was beadwork on the shanks of both the engagement ring and the wedding ring "jacket," which was four round diamonds that fit around the engagement ring. She wore the rings for special occasions and had another wedding band for every day.

She actually had lost that wedding band for a while. It had come from an estate sale and was very beautiful and unusual. She was devastated when she couldn't find it. It must have been caught on the bedsprings because it suddenly appeared under the bed about four months later. Of course, she was astounded and absolutely thrilled.

My mother did not have a lot of expensive jewelry, but she had a lot of costume jewelry. She was a teacher and wore mostly costume jewelry to work and around the neighborhood.

After my mother passed in 1986 my sister-in-law June and I got together to divide up her jewelry. At the time, unlike today, you either wore white or yellow jewelry and did not mix them, except for engagement and wedding rings. You could own both colors but only wore one color at a time. The book *Color Me Beautiful*, first published in 1973, was a guide to your color pallet according to your skin tone, hair color, and other factors and was all the rage. Everyone became a season. I was Spring and yellow gold jewelry was for me.

We sat at my father's dinette table and made three piles of jewelry, one for her, one for me and one to give to my cousin to sell at a flea market. He got all the costume earrings, as my mother did not have pierced ears and we both did, plus all of the pieces that we both rejected.

It so happened that June liked white. The exception was that my father chose to give my mother's engagement ring set and a few other diamond pieces to me, as well as most of my grandmother's jewelry that my mother had inherited.

It was very easy. No arguments, just a nice division.

I had my own wedding rings, several of them as a matter of fact; and I took my mother's and grandmother's rings and put them in my bank vault until I decided what to do with them. And there they stayed.

One day I happened to be looking in the vault for some papers when I came across the rings. I realized that my mother had now been gone 25 years and no one was enjoying the rings except the vault. I opened the box and realized that I really loved the set my husband had made for my mother and there was no reason why I shouldn't be enjoying it. I took it out of the vault and decided that since I still have my other wedding rings, I would do what my mother did and wear her set on special occasions.

I realized that it was not my mother's set anymore. It was mine, and I have been happily enjoying it for eight years.

Contributed by Janet Metz Walter

PASSING THE JEWELRY

There are several stories shared here. They all involve family traditions and jewelry that have been passed down through my family.

1- The story starts with my mother, a Holocaust survivor who grew up in Vienna. There, she had a boyfriend; but unfortunately, they were separated when her family immigrated to the Lower East Side of New York, not far from what is now The Tenement Museum, and his family moved to Australia. Before parting, he gave my mother a beautiful silver pin to remember him. My mother always kept this pin.

I loved it and, as a child, when my mother left for work in the morning, I would take the pin from its hiding place and wear it to school. Then I'd put it back as soon as I got home before my mother returned. That was a little rambunctious, and I guess I was very lucky that I never lost it.

2- While my father was in the Army, his hobby was making jewelry out of coins. He shaped them into hearts and made a bracelet and a ring which he intended to give to the woman he would someday marry but hadn't yet met. My mother was the lucky woman who got the jewelry.

3- My grandmother had a plain gold wedding band that I inherited after she died. In the Jewish religion, you are supposed to get married in a plain band with no cuts, stones, or designs on it to symbolize a smooth, solid, eternal marriage. I got married wearing that ring and then started a tradition of every child in the family using that wedding band in their marriage ceremonies. Both of my children and my brother's wife got married using that ring. When the ceremony is over and the bride is wearing her own wedding band, I take the ring back and put it away. I hope that someday I will be able to give it to my grandchildren for their wedding ceremonies.

4 - Another piece of jewelry that I keep for special occasions is a mezuzah that belonged to my mom. I wore it when I had special school exams, my Masters Degree exams, Occupational Therapy license exam, and my thesis defense. It was worn by my children and grandchildren for their special events such as Bris and Baby Naming.

When my son was a baby, he actually managed to bite into it; and it now has a little baby tooth mark in it. Recently I was going to give it to my granddaughter to wear for her Bat Mitzvah, but I decided instead to give her my diamond Chai pendant as a gift for her to keep.

5 - I inherited a box of jewelry from my parents when they passed away, unfortunately way too young. I hadn't realized that when my father bought my mother a gold bracelet, he had also bought the same one for my grandmother. I gave the box to a girlfriend of mine to hold when I went on a trip to Hawaii. When I came home and opened the box, I found the two bracelets. I asked my girlfriend if she had the same bracelet and accidentally put it into that box. She said she had not put anything into the box and that the two bracelets must have been there the whole time.

When I realized who had owned the two bracelets, I gave one to my sister-in-law on the night before her wedding and I kept one for myself. I wrote a note to my sister-in-law telling her that we both now shared my father's love for the two women he loved most in his life.

Contributed by Eileen S

HONORING GREAT GRANDMA

My mother has an earring and necklace set that belonged to my great grandmother. They are antique drop diamond post earrings in a silver octagon setting. There are two drops on the earrings and three drops on the matching necklace.

Eventually, the set was passed down to my grandmother who is still alive; but my mother became the keeper of the jewelry.

Obviously, it is very old and my mother keeps it in a special place and wears it occasionally.

My mother decided that she would let me wear them on special occasions. The first time I borrowed the set, my mother put the earrings in my ears and the necklace around my neck and took them off when I came back from the event. She then put them away again.

This became a tradition. I never touch the jewelry. My mom puts it on me and takes it off me every time.

Eventually, sometime in the future, it will be passed on to me. Until then, I am very happy to honor my great grandmother, my grandmother and my mother by letting my mother be the keeper.

The below picture shows my great grandmother holding me for the first time. She is wearing the earrings and necklace. The picture was given to me by my grandmother the last time I visited her.

You can't see the jewelry too well but it is an honor to share the picture, and there is another close-up picture of the jewelry.

Anonymous

SURVIVOR RING

My family came from the Czech Republic. My grandparents had five daughters.

My aunt was born in 1916 and was sent to America at the age of 16 to stay with an uncle when people were starting to be persecuted.

She carried a ring to America. It belonged to her mother, my grandmother, and turned out to be the only piece of family jewelry that survived.

As the Nazis took control of the city, my grandmother put her jewelry inside jars of grape jelly. The Nazis came into the house and searched everything. They opened the jars of jelly and found the jewelry. They took it and slapped my grandfather with their hands full of jelly, mostly on his face and into his beard.

The ring in America was the only piece of jewelry that they didn't get.

Eventually, the family wound up in Auschwitz. My grandparents and one of the five sisters were killed. The other three sisters volunteered to work in the kitchen. They made a pact that if one was killed the other two would volunteer to go with her so they would always be together.

As it turned out, the three surviving sisters came to New York to be with their sister in Brooklyn. They were so happy to be reunited that they decided to make copies of the ring their sister had. They had the rings mounted on pendants containing seven birthstones representing the family members, one for each of them and each exactly the same.

No one knew which one was the original ring. The back of the pendant was inscribed, "Our Mom 1897."

My mother loved and appreciated her life in Brooklyn. She married my dad and had a happy life in New York, eventually moving to Long Island and acquiring new jewelry.

Her favorite piece was a gold bangle bracelet that she always wore. During her last sickness, when she needed surgery, she refused to let doctors remove the bangle bracelet. She cried and thrashed and screamed. We explained that she was a survivor and had lost everything in life. This was something she obviously needed to keep as she remembered that time in her life. Eventually, the doctors let her keep it on.

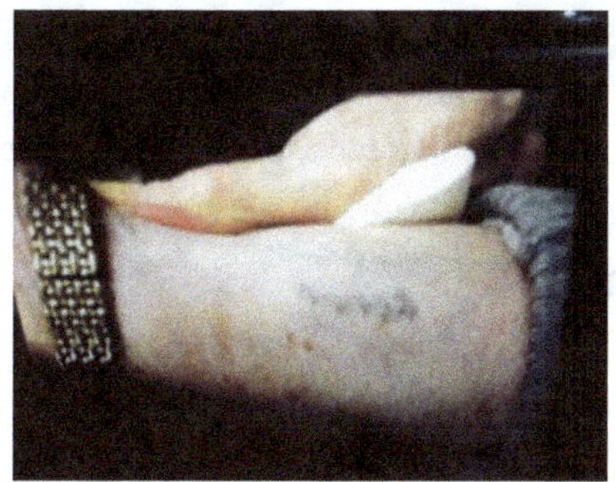

Clara's Holocaust Camp Tattoo

The accompanying pictures are of the pendant, front and back and of my beautiful mother Clara Markowitz Mermelstein wearing her pendant.

Contributed by Sandra Mermelstein Weissman

Author's note

Sandy was recommended to me for a story by another contributor who is a good friend of hers.

I happen to have cousins in my family whose name was originally

Mermelstein. My cousin had married into the family and her children were part of a very large family with that name. It was a very common name in Czechoslovakia; however, when I saw a picture of Sandy I realized that she looked very much like one of my cousins. Sandy and my cousins did not know each other.

After much texting, phone calls and research, we found out that Sandy is indeed a relative of my cousins. If I was not writing this book, they would never have found each other.

GIFTS FOR TWO SISTERS

My mother inherited a pair of antique earrings between 75 and 100 years old that may have even belonged to my great grandmother. They were fairly long and my mother decided to make them into two pendants, one for me and one for my sister.

We were at a family party out of town when my sister discovered that her pendant was missing. We searched everywhere for it but could not find it.

I would love to have the pendant duplicated to give it to my sister as a gift, but it would have to be exactly the same. I am now investigating the possibility and cost of doing that. I really would like her to have her matching pendant.

Anonymous

Chapter Five

LOST AND FOUND

Such a popular topic. I could have written the entire book about jewelry that was lost, some forever, and jewelry that was found again. Some of the stories are similar but each has a slightly different twist. Do any of them sound familiar?

WASHED OUT

When I was in Junior High School (what is now called Middle School), I had an opportunity to pick out a birthday gift for myself. It was a very special occasion for me. I picked out a gold and aquamarine birthstone ring that became very sentimental to me because of the circumstances of my getting this gift.

One day I realized that I could not find it. I was sad and miserable about it and so was my mother. She was always sad and upset for me when I was upset.

Not too long afterward, my mother was doing the laundry. There was a hose attached to the washing machine that drained the water out of the machine and into the sink. By some chance, my mother was in the laundry room at the time. I will never know why she happened to be watching the water come out of the hose; but suddenly, she noticed the ring come out of the hose with the water into the sink. Obviously, it must have either been in a pocket or got caught in the clothing as I was taking it off and putting in the laundry.

She jumped quickly to get the ring before it went down the drain. I will always remember that moment.

She was so excited that she was able to rescue it, and I was very touched by how happy she was. It proved how much she loved me.

I lost my mom when I was 31, and I still tear up thinking about how thrilled she was for me that she was able to catch the ring.

Contributed by Carol Leitner

I belong to several organizations that run events such as Auctions, Penny Socials, and Commemorative events that require raffle prizes. I often go through my store of unused gifts or prizes that I have won and donate them back as raffle prizes for an event.

At some point in time, I had acquired a jewelry cleaning machine; and although I wasn't using it for cleaning, it seemed like a good place to store the special occasion jewelry that I did not wear every day.

One day when asked for a prize donation, I came across the machine and decided that since I wasn't using it, it would be a nice prize to donate.

I totally forgot that I had hidden all of my special jewelry inside the machine. I had done it a while ago and I guess I did not have an occasion where I needed the jewelry.

I brought the machine to the organization running the event.

On the night before the event, I got a call from the chairperson of the event asking me if I knew that all my jewelry was in the machine.

I was totally shocked. I couldn't believe what she was telling me and that I had actually forgotten about it.

What's more, having run many of these events myself, I knew that not every prize is carefully inspected if it is new and in a box or wrapping of some kind. It just happened that someone was looking at the machine and deciding how to display it.

The scenarios were endless:

The person who discovered the jewelry could have taken it.

They may not have remembered who donated it.

The person who won the machine could have kept it.

The person who won the machine could have put it away to use as a gift for someone else or as a prize for another organization.

The jewelry could have spent months or years in a closet and when finally discovered no one would have had any idea who it might have belonged to. Who knows if they would have called the organization to find out. I would like to think that they would.

In any case, I will be eternally grateful to the person who discovered it and was honest and kind enough to call me and let me know that she had it and that I could come and get it back.

Contributed by Ellen K.

The year I turned 40 was also my 20th Anniversary.

I had a cousin who was a jeweler, and he made me up a beautiful diamond wedding band for my combination present from my husband.

My parents lived close by and we visited them often, going for dinner on Friday evenings and helping them shop and run other errands.

They had a closet in their apartment where they kept various things like cleaning supplies, paper towels, the vacuum cleaner, and luggage. On a shelf that was easy to reach were a few keys, like extra house keys and a key to their neighbor's apartment. He actually borrowed it a few times when he forgot his own key or had locked himself out when he ran out with the garbage.

Under the shelf was a supermarket plastic bag where we stored other bags to use for both garbage and for me to take home leftovers from dinner. When we came home from shopping, I would fold up the bags and place them in the "storage" bag. When we needed a new garbage bag or take-home bag, we would take it from the bag in the closet.

One day I noticed that my diamond wedding ring was missing. I could not figure out where it could have fallen off my finger. I looked frantically everywhere I could think of in my own apartment, in the car, among my clothing, and even in my parents' apartment. I could not find it and I believed that I must have lost it in a store or a restaurant or some other place where I would never find it. I had no idea where to even think of looking.

I was so upset over the loss of the ring and how careless I believed I was that I actually stopped wearing any jewelry at all; and it had been my habit to wear multiple rings, necklaces, and other jewelry. At times I wore a ring on almost every finger. Now I put them away and refused to wear any.

About six months later when I was at my parents' house for a usual visit, my mother handed me a box. I asked her what it was and she told me to open it. Inside was my wedding ring! I couldn't believe my eyes! I asked her where she had found it. She told me the story!

She had gone one day to the closet shelf to give her neighbor his extra key, as he had forgotten his. It was not on the shelf. Frantically, she started checking all of the folded plastic bags inside the bag underneath the shelf to see if it had fallen into the storage bag or between the bags that were folded up. When she was almost at the bottom, she picked up a bag and something rattled. She thought it was the key; but to her surprise, it turned out to be my ring.

My mother had forgotten that she had moved the keys to a safer place in a drawer.

It was something that was meant to be.

If she had remembered that she had moved the keys, my ring would probably have been thrown out in a bag that was used for garbage. It might have stayed in the bottom of the storage bag forever since everybody kept piling new bags on top of the few bags that were at the bottom. The ring must have fallen off my finger and landed inside the bag that I was folding to store in the other bag. It was amazing that no one got to the bottom of the storage bag in six months.

I was so astounded and relieved I not only started wearing the ring again but also started wearing all the other jewelry that I had put away and had not worn in six months.

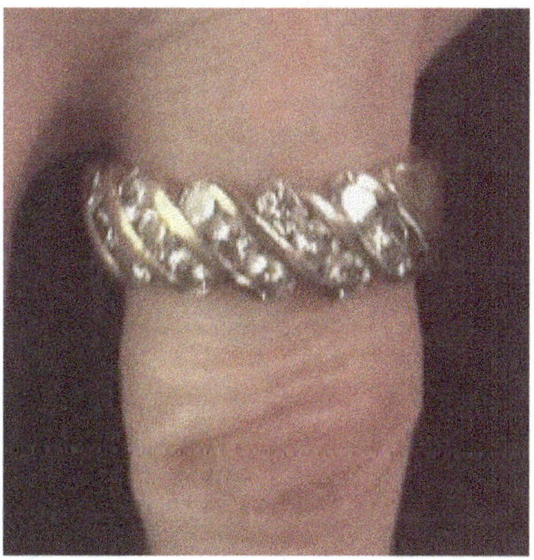

Contributed by Janet Levine

THE MYSTERIOUS WATCH DISAPPEARANCE

My parents bought me a beautiful watch with diamonds around the face for my 30th birthday. They had it engraved on the back saying "with love from Mom and Dad."

One weekend, my family and I stayed in the city at the Waldorf Hotel. I dressed up nicely and wore the watch.

When we woke up the next day, I could not find the watch. In a panic, I searched high and low and realized the watch was gone. I could not figure out what had happened to it. We looked everywhere—under the bed, in the bathroom, on the chairs and desk, in the drawers. The watch had disappeared into thin air.

We were going to a wedding the next weekend and we were taking my parents with us. I knew my dad would expect me to wear the watch! I had a panic attack.

My husband ran to Manhattan and after running from one store to another he found the exact watch, but there was no time to engrave it.

My parents came by as I was getting dressed for the wedding. I wore the watch and took a deep breath. No one said a word and I believed that everything was fine.

Fifteen years later, yes fifteen, we were packing to go on vacation and I brought up several suitcases from the basement. As I dropped a suitcase on the floor, the original watch with the engraved message on the back fell out. I gasped. For fifteen years the watch was safely hidden in a pocket of that suitcase. The most amazing part was that we still owned the suitcase after fifteen years.

The next time I saw my parents, I told my dad about the watch. He told me he knew all these years that that was the wrong watch because he saw it on my dresser the night of the wedding, picked it up, and when he turned it around it wasn't engraved.

How thoughtful and sweet he was to keep it to himself and not upset or embarrass me by telling me that he knew.

I guess at some point I could have had the second watch engraved, but I never bothered since I didn't think anyone knew the difference.

I ended up giving the "new" watch to my mother and keeping the original engraved watch.

Contributed by Marilyn M

TRUSTWORTHY CLEANERS

I have been working as a legal assistant for a large New York City law firm for over 40 years. I became pregnant with my second son, 32 years ago.

Before I started wearing maternity clothes, on this particular day, I was wearing a blazer. My fingers were a little swollen and my engagement ring was a little tight on my finger, so I took the ring off and put it in the pocket of the blazer.

I then decided it was time to put away my regular business clothes and start wearing maternity clothes, so I took all of my business clothes to the cleaners so that they would all be clean and pressed when I was ready to wear them again. I totally forgot that the ring was in the pocket of the blazer.

When I realized what had happened, I just assumed that the ring was gone, either in a cleaning machine or in the possession of the lucky person who found it. I was fairly sure that no one had admitted to finding it; otherwise, I would have gotten a phone call. I knew I wasn't going to replace the ring until after the baby was born.

I picked up the clothes in their cleaning plastic a few days later and put them away in a closet, very sad about losing my ring, but I had something else to be excited about.

Six months later after my son was born and I was going back to work, I took out my business clothes and just out of curiosity I stuck my hand in the pocket of the blazer when I removed it from the cleaning plastic. In the pocket was a note saying that the owner had the ring and to please call him. I was so shocked, I couldn't believe that I had never thought to check the pocket when I got the cleaning back.

I called the owner and he said to me "I thought you would never call. When I found the ring I put it in my mother's vault for safekeeping. You can come and pick it up tomorrow."

I have no idea why he did not call me right away, maybe he didn't want his employees to hear; but I was still very impressed with this honest, trustworthy man. Now I had two things to celebrate: my beautiful new baby and the return of my ring!

Contributed by Karen F.

THANKS, PARTNER

I am a physician, and I had recently moved to a new office with my colleague. Married at that time for thirty years, I always wore my wedding and engagement rings together. My engagement ring was very simple: a diamond in a plain, standard gold setting. One day as I was working in the office, I noticed that my hand momentarily got snagged on my pants, but I disregarded it.

Several hours later when I was done examining patients, I noticed that I had no diamond in my ring. In a panic, I started searching the office for the stone. I did not see it anywhere. I looked in the exam rooms, the bathroom and throughout the office. I looked for over an hour.

I had been to the dentist earlier that day and had her check her office, to no avail. I ran to the parking lot, searching the elevator and the lobby along the way, following my route to the car. Nothing.

By then the sun had set, and I borrowed a flashlight in hopes of seeing the glitter of a diamond on the tarmac. Still nothing. I had to go home and tell my husband what had happened. It was so sad!

I was dejected returning to the office the next morning. I was the first one there; and fortunately, the cleaning people had not yet arrived.

When my partner Dr. G came in, I told him the story. Seeing how upset I was, he said he would take another look around. Dr. G didn't tell me, but he thought that he could use his peripheral vision to look for the diamond and concentrate not only on what he saw in front of him but also on his sides! A few minutes later he came over to me and told me to hold out my hand. I did and he dropped the diamond into it. I was awestruck! He had spotted something shiny in his peripheral vision on the floor near the leg of my desk. All the time I had spent searching, all the places I looked, and he came up with it in a few minutes. I was so relieved I broke into tears and started to hug him. He held me for a minute, and when I stepped away from him his shirt was all wet. I could not thank him enough.

My husband knew a jeweler that he had dealt with and had him make up a whole new setting for the ring which was sturdier, with stronger prongs. It is the ring I still wear.

I learned that with diamond rings, it is possible for prongs to loosen and bend. I assume that's what happened when my hand brushed against and caught on my pants. I now realize that rings should be checked every once in a while to make sure there are no loose or broken prongs or that the stone is well seated. Using a jeweler that you know and trust to set the ring properly is also a must.

I always knew I was blessed to work with Dr. G, and the events of that day underlined how lucky I have been—I will never be able to thank my partner enough for finding my diamond!

Contributed by Dr. Mary J

AN EMERALD NECKLACE AND A TODDLER . . . WHAT COULD GO WRONG?

When my daughter Kathleen was born, my husband gifted me with a beautiful necklace with an emerald Claddagh surrounded by a circle of diamonds. Our daughter Kathleen was born in May, so this beautiful necklace captured both her Irish heritage and name along with her birthstone.

A Claddagh is a traditional Irish symbol which looks like a heart wearing a crown with hands on each side. It symbolizes love, loyalty and friendship, as the hands represent friendship, the heart represents love, and the crown represents loyalty.

I wore it constantly, and had it on a sturdy chain, as I had a very "grabby" baby who was always pulling on me. Well, that baby learned to walk - and talk! - and one day when I was resting on the couch my daughter asked to wear my necklace. I was tired - and pregnant - and thought (very foolishly!!!) "What could possibly go wrong?" as I fastened the necklace around her neck.

She toddled into the kitchen, returned mere seconds later, and the necklace was gone! I jumped up and searched everywhere - the kitchen, the garbage, the drawers - even her diaper over the next several days! - but the necklace was gone.

Months later my husband gutted the entire kitchen for a renovation right down to the studs, but the necklace never materialized. I can't even imagine what could have happened! My daughter is now a grown woman, and it still remains the biggest mystery ever!

Contributed by Stephanie L.

OH NO! NOT AGAIN!

Many years ago my wife was trying on coats in a store. Her diamond ring caught in the sleeve and she heard the stone drop to the floor. She frantically searched all over but was unable to find it. Other people helped her search, but supposedly no one saw it.

The ring was insured so I called the insurance company. The adjuster told me that I needed to supply concrete proof that the stone was really lost. What more concrete proof could we provide other than the stone was not in the ring, she heard it drop, and if we had it we would have put it back into her ring? Surprisingly, he denied the claim which was rather obnoxious. After all, that's the reason you have insurance. We went back and forth about what the next step was and he suggested going to court. I offered to split the amount of the settlement rather than taking it to court and he said "probably not," so I said, "OK, I will see you in court."

I guess he wasn't expecting that response, or perhaps he spoke with his superior; but in any case, he called the next morning with a compromise agreement. So we replaced the stone in the ring.

Believe it or not, just one year later, she lost the new one, as well! This time I didn't even bother calling the insurance company.

We eventually found out that the setting was defective and was not holding the stone correctly. I guess I could have sued the jeweler; but it was a difficult case to prove, especially since it could have been damaged when it got caught on the sleeve of the coat.

We came to the conclusion that she was not meant to have that ring. Instead, she had a ring of her mother's which was what she decided to wear instead.

Contributed by Elliott S. and Harriet S.

JEWISH STAR

y husband had bought me a Jewish Star pendant from Tiffany.

One day I went to wear it and could not find it. Of course, I was very upset and I looked all over for it.

Then I panicked because I did not want my husband to know that I had lost it.

I decided to go to Tiffany to see if they had the same one, and I would replace it and he would never know.

I had no idea how much he had paid for it; but when I got to Tiffany, I realized that it was much more money than I was willing to spend to replace it. I did not know whether to just tell him or try to find another one that looked similar.

I shopped around a little and finally decided to go to a Judaica store. I found a very similar star and bought it in hopes that he would never notice the difference.

He never mentioned it, and I don't know if he never noticed or just decided not to say anything. Obviously, he had to know that I cared enough to try to replace it if he did notice.

After a while, the first star turned up in a place where I had never thought to look. I don't know if I put it there for a reason or if I just put it there temporarily and forgot about it, but now I have two very similar star pendants.

I'm so glad that I didn't spend a fortune on a replacement at Tiffany's since the original did turn up.

Contributed By Helen K

Chapter Six

REPURPOSED JEWELRY

This is the sister chapter to Inheritance. What do you do when you inherit a piece of jewelry that has sentimental value but you really don't care for it or have no use for it?
See what the people in these stories did. Maybe it will give you ideas. And then you can consult with us to get it done.

GRANDMA'S GIGANTIC JEWELS

My grandfather grew up in Hell's Kitchen, a neighborhood in New York City. He became a CPA and was very successful.

When he and my grandmother got married, they lived in the city and traveled extensively. My grandmother also traveled with her sister. She cruised on the Queen Mary and traveled to various places in Asia where she found some jewelers that she connected with and started buying jewelry.

My grandmother was a big lady with large hands and fingers, and she bought large stones that she had made into rings and other jewelry. She developed such a love for her jewelry that she would buy stones in all colors so that she had a set of jewelry to match every outfit.

My grandparents often went to Atlantic City, and my grandmother found a place there where she always bought diamonds. I fell in love with a diamond and sapphire ring and "visited" it on her finger whenever I saw her. It contained a three and a half-carat diamond, a four-carat sapphire, and 14 baguettes. She promised me that someday it would be mine along with some earrings. My ears weren't pierced at that time and before I had them done at age 35, a cleaning lady helped herself to the box of earrings.

The jewelry was spectacular and over the top. It was perfect for my grandmother; but when it came time for her to give it away or when it was divided among family members after she passed, not everyone wanted or needed such overwhelming jewelry. My mother was a very modest person and did not really want any of the jewelry; however, everybody including my mother got pearls. There were also two sapphire and diamond bangle bracelets. I received one of them. My sister received an ornate ruby bracelet.

My grandmother gave me the diamond and sapphire ring several years before she passed, and I spent time thinking about how I could repurpose it for myself. I loved it but could never wear it the way it was. I took the diamond out and had a new engagement ring made for myself by a well-known jeweler on Long Island. Most notably, I took the baguettes from the original ring along with several stones from other jewelry and made a heart necklace that was embedded with all those stones.

My original engagement ring had a diamond that my grandfather had sold to my fiancé. It came from a stick pin. Another stick pin became a necklace that matched my new engagement ring.

The one stone I never repurposed was the sapphire from the original ring. I hope to find a place for it someday.

Contributed by Barbara W.

SPECTACULAR CREATIONS

My mother owned a lot of diamond jewelry, including stud earrings, her engagement ring, wedding ring, and various other pieces that had smaller diamonds in them. Before she died, she wanted to make sure that her jewelry wouldn't be lost or sold or given to anyone else, so she gave it all to me.

I had no idea what to do with the amazing abundance of diamonds that I was given. I decided that I was going to take all of the diamonds and make them into a special piece as a remembrance of her.

I designed an intriguing ring from her stud earrings and an array of smaller diamonds and took all of her other stones and made a breathtaking pendant that I call "Heart of the Ocean." The center stone is her pear shape, and both the pendant and chain contain an assortment of other diamonds.

They are both spectacular pieces; and although they were designed by me and made up for me, I will always think of my mother whenever I wear them.

Contributed by Robin B

MY IN-LAWS' GIFTS

I had the good fortune of having a very nice relationship with my in-laws and still do with my mother-in-law.

Many years ago my mother-in-law decided that she would like me to have a very valuable old diamond necklace of hers. I appreciated the gift but was really not thrilled with the style, and she kindly gave me permission to repurpose it into something that I would be happy to wear. I had it made into a modern bezel set necklace.

I had an insurance rider for my jewelry and was waiting for an appraisal of the remade necklace when our house was robbed and every single piece of jewelry I owned was taken. I was not only stunned, devastated, and every other synonym you can imagine but also upset that I did not have an up-to-date appraisal to give the insurance company. To console me, my mother-in-law very generously gave me a diamond tennis bracelet. At least I would have something to wear and enjoy.

About twenty years later, a few weeks after my birthday, we were at my great nephew's birthday party. I thanked my father-in-law for the birthday check he had sent me and he said: "We actually have something else for you." At that point, my mother-in-law handed me a ring. She told me that my father-in-law wanted me to have it while he was still alive. My family actually describes it as hideous, but I wore it all that day and showed everyone my gift.

In fact, we have no idea when he gave my mother-in-law that ring but I had never seen her wear it. My sister-in-law had worked for a jewelry company and had gotten them the ring years before. My kids laughed about how ugly it was, but you can't account for someone else's taste. No one said anything to my father-in-law about what they thought of the ring.

My father-in-law must have had a sense that he was dying when he gave it to me; and he, in fact, passed a few weeks later. My mother-in-law told me to wear it for a while and not reset it, but it was way too big on me anyway. When I spoke to my sister-in-law she laughed and told me to "ignore Mom—she NEVER wore it! Just go ahead and reset it."

I had it reset shortly after my father-in-law passed and showed it to Mom who was very happy.

I now wear the ring every day. It serves as a special memory of my father-in-law and the wonderful relationship we had.

Anonymous

THE WATCH BRACELET AND OTHER PIECES

*O*verall, my approach to a piece of jewelry is that I smile and even giggle to myself when I am wearing it because it reconnects me to family memories—and wider history—how times and styles have changed.

The watch piece admittedly looks a little grubby, but we all would at 150 years, and I love having those many years around my wrist. The piece actually consists of four watches.

I was thrilled when my granddaughter Harper's father, our son, gave me the picture watch and crushed when it stopped; but with three old-timers dormant in my jewelry box, I had the idea that I could make a happy one piece out of four "unfixables."

My jeweler went for the idea even though she could not clean the Tiffany's face. To me, it is a sort of a joke piece. I think it is pretty funny looking but carries a lot of sentimentality and memories with it. I wear it when life is informal, so more and more now. I love it, particularly because each watch has an engraving on the back.

1. The Tiffany: MCS—Margaret Clark Sessions. My father's parents gave it to my mother as a wedding present. It brings her back to me, and I picture it on her wrist always with a black grosgrain ribbon strap.

2. SHS: One-eyed, great Aunt Sarah Sears Harkness who gave it to her daughter who gave it to me. Aunt Sarah lost that eye when her brother chased her around the dining room table with a stick which went into her eye—lesson learned.

3. Kate Wood: The Seiko which my husband had for me at the breakfast table on our 30th anniversary as our children gathered in some kind of amazement. (Next anniversary #62.)

4. The Harper face with her and her siblings' birth dates on the back. I will eventually give this to Harper and she may think it is a bad joke.

The Sunburst, "The Bijou" Pin

I think this was a wedding present from my grandfather's parents to my grandmother in 1902.

When I sat at the end of my mother's bed and watched her put the "Bijou" on, as my father called it, I thought she was like a queen. Every once in a while I would go into the bottom of my mother's closet to take a sneak peek. Then when the time came for the Bijou to be mine, I was embarrassed to wear it. It would seem as though I was showing off.

What to do? Tone it down a bit. Another consultation with the jeweler and we had the answer. Replacing the outside diamonds with garnets worked for me. Now my daughter and I share it and it won't surprise me if someday it dresses down a pair of jeans. In my mind, it is my sports Bijou. With a family of boys, the traded diamonds helped a couple of engagement rings along.

The Chinese Jade and Stick Pins

My father was a fastidious dresser, not a flashy one. He wore stick pins with his ties, and he was known for that. After he died it made me sad to see those stick pins hanging out at the bottom of my jewel box. His grandsons loved his stick pins but were not going to wear them. My jeweler liked my idea of setting off the jade pin with the stick pins on the edges, and I love wearing the pin with more nostalgia than I had expected.

I think of my father's Chinese client who gave me the pin as a wedding present, I think of being 5 years old and struggling with chopsticks when we had to go to his home for a meal. I think of the Mah Jongg tips his wife with the very long red fingernails might give me if she were coaching me today, and I think of watching my father choosing his stick pin for the day.

Contributed by Kate Wood

JEWELRY MAKEOVERS

I had some jewelry that I inherited from family members.

One piece was a pin from my grandmother. It was yellow and white gold, with a blue stone in the center. I loved it, but it was small and I was afraid of losing it. I decided to consult a jeweler from New York City who also had a place in Rye Brook, NY. His wife was skilled at repurposing jewelry, so I went up there to see her.

The jeweler connected each side of the pin to a beautiful chain set with diamonds and made a choker out of the pin. Every time I wear it, someone stops me to admire it.

I then decided to refashion some of my old jewelry pieces. Although I didn't wear them often, I did not want to part with them either. They were gifts accumulated through the years—thick herringbone chains, assorted necklaces, and pendants, charms and bracelets—all 14K or 18K gold.

My cousin in Israel has a friend who makes jewelry. She melts down old gold pieces and makes new pieces out of the gold. I brought the jewelry with me on a trip to Israel to have her see what could be done. She had a collection of pieces to pick from, and I looked online to find things that I liked. When my cousin saw the jewelry, she laughed and said they were outdated from the '80s—frozen in time. That made it easier for me to part with them. I had her friend melt the pieces down and had them remade into necklaces and earrings that I now enjoy wearing.

One piece of jewelry that I still have and will not alter is an onyx ring. It is a rectangular stone on a white gold setting with a diamond in the center. It was given to my mom for her elementary school graduation in 1929. It was a pretty sophisticated gift for a young girl, but my mother had a cousin in the jewelry business who gave it to her when she graduated. I never changed or touched it. I was even afraid to leave it with a jeweler when the stone was loose.

The picture is of my mom wearing the ring. It makes me happy every time I look at it.

Contributed by Ellen W

Chapter Seven

UP ABOVE

Some people are very big believers that there is a hereafter. Many people either don't believe or are afraid to believe. Are our relatives and friends looking down on us and guiding us or is it all in our heads? These stories will make you think about that.

A few years ago I was heading into the city on the LIRR to celebrate a friend's 50th birthday. A fun couple of days was planned. Upon sitting down on the train, I noticed in a pure panic that the diamond from my engagement ring was gone. All that was left were the prongs. I couldn't believe it. I quickly looked through my things as best I could, being that I was on the train; but there was no diamond.

I arrived in the city, met my girlfriend, and we headed over to our hotel. I didn't want to ruin her birthday celebration, but all I could think about was that diamond—you see, it was my husband's grandmother's diamond that had so graciously been handed down to me.

When we got to the hotel I immediately called my husband to tell him the news. He was so understanding, knowing how upset I was, and reassured me that is what insurance was for and I shouldn't worry.

Of course, this put a damper on our girl's NYC adventure, but I tried to enjoy it. Our last day there we went to my son's apartment where he had a pool on the roof of his building. This was the middle of June and we were going to take advantage of a beautiful day and sit by the pool. I put my bathing suit on, headed up to the roof, and went into my straw beach bag to grab my towel. IT WAS A MIRACLE—sitting on the bottom of the straw bag was the diamond. I was in shock and couldn't believe that I actually found it. My mother-in-law was absolutely looking down on me!!

As soon as I arrived home, we went straight to the jeweler to have the diamond remounted—so grateful that the diamond was miraculously found and never really lost in the first place.

Contributed by Dee G

THE AMETHYST PENDANT

I have never been a big believer in psychics or mediums or talking to people who have passed, but there are a couple of stories that have sometimes made me wonder if someone is really looking down on us and sending messages.

My mother's birthday was in February so she had several pieces of amethyst jewelry that I inherited when she passed. She had always taken care of her brother, who was somewhat learning disabled, had been married and divorced in the early '50s, and had no children. After he got divorced, he moved back in with my grandparents. When they passed, my parents looked after him.

After both of our parents had passed, my brother and I took over the care of our uncle. At some point in time, we realized that he could not live alone anymore; and we put him into an assisted living facility. The facility was not far from me, and I visited him fairly often. He had been there several years when I decided to drop by one day. I had had a very busy day putting in a few hours as a volunteer at a Bingo game. I was wearing purple that day and had my mother's small gold and amethyst pendant on my neck.

I had put on a coat, driven from my house, run around the room where Bingo was being held for about five hours, put my coat back on, walked through the parking lot, and driven to the assisted living facility.

I met my uncle in the all-purpose room and after visiting a while he informed me that he couldn't find his glasses. We took the elevator up to his room, and I searched his dresser drawers for his glasses. I found the glasses and turned to the task of hanging up and putting away laundry that had been returned to his room and was on the bed.

At some point, I spotted something shiny right in the middle of his bedroom floor. I assumed it was a piece of glitter or shiny paper that had come from a party downstairs. When I went to pick it up, it was the amethyst pendant! I had not felt it fall off the chain, and I couldn't believe what I was seeing. I felt the chain around my neck and; sure enough, there was no pendant there. After all of the places that I had been to that day, I could not fathom that the pendant hadn't fallen off until we got to his room. I would have been heartbroken if I had lost it.

Despite that I usually don't believe, I somehow felt that this had to be my mother's way of thanking me for taking care of her brother.

Contributed by Janet Metz Walter

THE HEART IN THE FISH BOWL

Unfortunately, I have lost three brothers in the past four years.

When my brother Joe died in 2015 on his anniversary, I decided that I wanted to get a little tattoo of a broken heart. My family talked me out of it because they said it was too sad of a reminder.

My brother Phil was a fishing fanatic and I went fishing with him a few times. I have a summer home in the Berkshires; and after Phil passed away a year after Joe, my sister decided to come up for a weekend. We went to a tag sale. I saw a fishbowl there that I thought would be a nice memento of Phil and his love of fishing. The fishbowl was decorated with sand and shells.

I left it on my porch table until we were ready to go home. I decided that I did not want the sand, so I took out the shells and emptied the sand into a container. Just before I was going to throw it away, I decided to rake my fingers through the sand to make sure there was nothing in there. I felt metal and found a silver heart locket with an old English B on the front. Here was my heart. My sister asked me what I would do with a locket that had a B on it. I told her it stood for "brothers."

Years ago I sold a ring that I'd found in my temple storage room. The temple had been rented to an outside group for a party. We had no idea who attended, but someone had apparently tried to get into the locked storage room which was missing its doorknob. The room was locked from the inside and only a few people were authorized to access it from behind the stage. The person had no business being there. As she apparently tried to find the lock through the hole, she must have dropped the small ring. I found it on the floor days later. There was no way of finding out to whom it belonged because certainly, no one would admit to trying to break into the room. So I kept the ring. I eventually sold it to a jeweler and bought a silver chain with the money. It was never used and had been kept in a drawer. Now I realized that the chain was waiting for a special partner. I used it for the locket that I wear around my neck all the time.

Last year my brother Frank died. Two days later I broke the fishbowl.

This year our temple merged with another one and the building, which was in disrepair, is being torn down. So the locket I wear around my neck is a reminder of my brothers and the temple where I was very active and had wonderful memories. My brother Frank was also active in the same temple.

I never took the heart off. We went on a cruise and one night, for the first time, I took off the silver chain and heart, as it didn't go with what I was wearing. There was no set seating on the small ship, so we were ushered to a large table. As we introduced ourselves, I had to laugh. Sitting to my right was Pat G and her husband Richard (brother number 4 is Richard). Across from us was Joe and Ann (My brother Joe, the oldest, was married to Marie G, the same last name but not related.) At this point, I asked if there was a Phil at the table. There was a Steve, but no Phil. Directly behind me, a man heard me ask and told me he was Phil! Of course, I had to explain the whole story to the other 10 people at the table, and I became friends with Pat G who lives near me.

Contributed by Lucille Siegel

THE PILL THAT SAVED THE BRACELET

On my 18th birthday, my parents gave me a gold link bracelet. I have worn it daily (except to sleep) for the last 36 years. It is part of who I am.

Several months ago when I arrived home, I noticed the bracelet was not on my wrist. The bracelet is fairly heavy, and I was sure I would have noticed if it had slipped off. I retraced my steps that day and returned to my office to search but to no avail. I went to the bank and Staples, as those were my only two other stops that day. I searched and inquired also with no luck. I was resolved that it was gone forever and even started my search to find an exact replacement. Although it would never be the same, it would represent what it meant to me.

About a week later, I was going to dinner with a friend. I had a slight headache and decided to take some Advil before I left the house. In an effort to not take the pill on an empty stomach, I went into the cabinet and grabbed the box of Wheat Thins. The box was virtually empty and I grabbed a few of the remaining broken crackers and took the pill. I didn't want to leave an empty box in the cabinet, so I took the box with me and was going to dispose of it in the trash can in the garage as I left. As I was placing the "empty" box in the trash, in an effort not to waste a single morsel, I reached again into the box to grab some of the crumbs. It was at that moment that I felt something odd. It was not a cracker, it was my bracelet!

Apparently, when reaching into the box a week earlier to grab a snack, the bracelet slid off my wrist. It was seconds from being gone forever. It had to be a higher power that had me take the box to the garage as opposed to putting it in the kitchen garbage and to have one last reach into the box to find the bracelet.

Miracles do happen.

Contributed by Mark

THE PROPOSAL FROM HEAVEN

When my son decided that he was going to ask his girlfriend to marry him, they were both still in law school at GWU in DC. They had met each other their first year and had become friends. The relationship morphed from classmates to friends to a couple. My son had a studio apartment in a condo near the school, and his girlfriend lived in Virginia.

When an apartment became available for rent in the building, she decided to move there. They basically lived in his apartment and used her apartment for studying and homework when they each needed to be alone to work. They also kept their out-of-season clothes there and all of their possessions that did not fit into his apartment. Finally, my son realized that this was the girl he wanted to marry and decided to start looking for a ring.

By this time people were wondering if it was going to happen. Even her grandmother asked us when he was going to propose when we all attended her mother's wedding to her second husband. (This took place in a temple in Lexington, Kentucky on a Saturday in June after we all watched the Belmont Stakes first on the TV set up in the lobby.) Coming from Long Island, I found that funny.

My son did not have far to go since his father Ken owned a jewelry business. He asked his father for a ring catalog and pretended that a friend had asked him to get it for him. He sat down with his girlfriend to casually look through the catalog before he gave it to his friend. He looked it over again by himself and chose the ring he wanted, a beautiful center stone with small round diamonds and baguettes on the sides. My husband did not even tell me this was happening.

When the ring was made up and my son got it, he arranged to take a break from studying on a Wednesday evening, the best evening for both of their schedules. He planned a picnic in her apartment downstairs as it had a little more free space. The date was October 20th. His idea was to set up a picnic basket of food and a tablecloth for the floor just like a real picnic in the park, hide the ring in the basket and then propose.

On Wednesday morning, her stepfather called and informed them that he was in town on business and wanted to meet them for dinner. My son was not a happy camper, he was kind of upset but he couldn't show it so, of course, he had to change his plan. He arranged the picnic for the next day, October 21st; and it was a beautiful, emotional proposal, and supposedly a total surprise to his girlfriend despite looking through the catalog.

My parents were both deceased, but October 21st happened to be the date of their wedding anniversary. It was such a fluke that it happened that way that I couldn't help but think that they were looking down from heaven and had arranged it to be on this date.

When my son and his new fiancee called us later that evening to announce their engagement which my husband, of course, knew about, his fiancee who knew very little about the jewelry business at the time breathlessly described the beautiful ring with the "dots and dashes" on the side of the center stone. That made all of us laugh and added to the happy occasion.

Contributed by Janet Metz Walter

EARRINGS FROM HEAVEN

*M*y first husband suddenly passed away in 1993 at age 49. I was 44, had two teenage children, and it was a totally devastating time in my life—one I was not prepared for, but then no one is.

Six months later, on the day that would have been my 23rd anniversary, my friends decided that I shouldn't be home thinking and grieving; and despite my protests, they finally convinced me to go out to dinner with them in Manhattan. We were down in The Village, and my friend knew of a little jewelry store there.

"Let's go in," she said. "You need to buy yourself a gift for your anniversary."

"I don't want a gift," I protested. "This is not a happy occasion for me." I was close to tears as my friends nudged me into the store. I wandered around as they did, and my dear friends suggested that I look at different pieces of jewelry. I couldn't convince them that I really was not thinking about jewelry.

Somewhere in my aimless wandering, I saw a little pair of earrings that I liked. My friends saw me looking at them and encouraged me to buy them. I actually saw two pairs of earrings that I liked. They were the same style but different colors, one gold and one mother of pearl. My friends tried to convince me to treat myself to both sets of earrings; but I decided that since I didn't plan on buying any, that one would be enough. It was definitely a treasured gift from my husband. When I made the decision to pay for them and went to the counter, I looked up at the cashier and saw something that to this day gives me chills. I saw a sign behind the counter with my husband's full name written out. When I could get the words out to ask her why his name was behind the counter on the wall, she told me he was the designer of this collection of earrings. His name was exactly the same! It was as if my husband was there and was telling me that I should buy the earrings as his gift to me. I was so stunned, I was shaking.

I decided to buy both sets of earrings, that it was meant for me to have them. My friends also couldn't believe their eyes. To me it was another sign that he was there, watching over us.

I now am happily remarried. I wore the pearl drops at my wedding. My husband was very understanding of the fact that I wore one of the pairs of earrings every day. Then I lost one of those pearl earrings, and I was grief- stricken. I keep the other one as a wonderful memory but still wear those little gold drops almost every day. It is my special way of remembering how lucky I was once, and how lucky I am again for a second time!!

Anonymous

GRANDMA'S MESSAGE

In the 1990's my husband and I moved from New York, to Ponce Inlet, Florida.

Ponce Inlet, in those days, was a quaint, sleepy fishing village at the end of an isthmus, south of Daytona Beach. It was remote and isolated with one road in, and one out, the ocean on one side and the Halifax River on the other.

Being used to having people around and in an unfamiliar place, I was nervous about being robbed, so I decided to hide my jewelry.

My grandmother had passed and left me some art deco onyx pieces, a solid gold bracelet watch and a sapphire and diamond spray brooch.

A few years passed and I decided to wear the onyx bracelet to a dance. I looked in my jewelry box and it wasn't there. After the panic, I remembered that I had secreted them away; but of course, I couldn't remember where.

My husband and I searched everywhere we could think they might be. I wracked my brain in the middle of the night, sleepless, trying to remember, and was sick about it. Time passed and I became resigned to the fact that the precious jewelry was lost.

Years later, my husband and I were divorcing and I was in the process of packing up my belongings to move back to New York. I packed numerous boxes and was cleaning out the coat closet when I saw a bag of rags I used for cleaning next to the vacuum. I went to toss it in the garbage and something told me to look through it. (Could it have been my grandmother?) Sure enough, in the bottom under all those rags, wrapped in a ripped white towel, was the blue velvet Crown Royal bag in which I always kept the jewelry.

My heart sank with disbelief. I had almost lost them forever, but in the next heartbeat, I was overwhelmed with joy and thankfulness.

At least something good came out of a very bad situation.

Contributed by Karen Constantine

Chapter Eight

TRAVEL STORIES

If you have visited any of these places you might be familiar with the settings of these stories. If you have not been to some or all of these places come with us for a visit.

By the time my husband and I were married two years, he had caught the travel bug; and we spent every vacation traveling. This particular summer we took a tour to Scandinavia. We were visiting Norway, Sweden, and Denmark and it was all breathtaking.

During some free time in Copenhagen, we were wandering down a street window shopping. We passed a jewelry store and decided to go in when I saw some interesting things in the window.

I fell in love with a ring that contained a domed amber stone set into a silver, flower pattern picture-frame setting. It was an unusual find for me because I usually did not combine brown or gold tones with silver. Yellow gold was much more popular at the time.

My husband bought me the ring and I enjoyed it for five years.

We eventually bought a house. I was pregnant and we were taking our time unpacking because we were busy redecorating the "handyman's special" that we purchased. We moved into the house in March.

In June I had a baby shower to go to in New Jersey, and my husband went along to spend the evening with his friend. I had an opal wedding ring that I still wear but left my engagement ring and matching wedding band in the dresser drawer along with a few other pieces of jewelry.

When we arrived home, we were startled and freaked out to find that someone had broken in while we were out for the evening. Whatever jewelry was in my bedroom drawer was stolen, which included the amber ring.

I was actually lucky that the majority of my jewelry was still at the bottom of a carton of books, but I was upset about the amber ring because I believed it could not be replaced. My husband replaced the engagement ring fairly quickly but I missed my amber ring.

Several years later, my parents were taking a trip to Scandinavia. It just happened that I still had the bill from the store where I bought the amber ring, just to keep as a reference in case we ever went back to Copenhagen.

I gave them the bill and described the ring and told them if they could find something similar to bring it back for me.

When they came home they handed me a box. They said that they hoped that what they found was as nice as the ring I had lost.

Inside the box was the exact same ring I had bought eight years before! And to this day I still wear it!

Contributed by Janet Metz Walter

SOME HISTORY AND AN UNEXPECTED FIND

A friend of mine owned a timeshare in Shawnee, Pennsylvania in the early 2000s. It is a very familiar spot to me because in the 1940s and '50s there was a choral group called "Fred Waring and the Pennsylvanians" that had a TV show and toured the country doing concerts. My uncle was the engineer and road manager for the group that was based in Shawnee.

Fred Waring purchased a golf resort well known for its tournaments, in 1943 and renamed it The Shawnee Inn. It became a mecca for celebrity visitors and golfers including Jackie Gleason, Lucille Ball, Art Carney, Ed Sullivan, and Perry Como, all well-known entertainers at the time. Arnold Palmer actually met his wife there.

It also happens that Fred Waring invented the Waring Blender, the precursor to the food processor.

My uncle lived near Shawnee, in Stroudsberg, so as a child I visited the area at least once a year with my family.

Eventually, in the 1970s part of the Waring property became the timeshare community; and The Shawnee Inn began to offer skiing. A whole new generation of people became enamored with Shawnee. My friend decided to invite a group of about 10 women up to the timeshare for a weekend, to partake in local activities and play Mah Jongg. We all were passionate players. Some friends from this group had taught others of us how to play years before; and eventually, I became a Mah Jongg teacher in an Adult Continuing Ed program.

We would set up two tables and play and gab and nosh until well after midnight. We always have a wonderful time together. The group changed from time to time as people moved away and other people joined. We have celebrated happy events together and helped each other through difficult and sad times. Several of the women have contributed stories to this book.

On these weekends, we shopped in the outlet mall and flea market, went to the casino and spa, and ate in the area's many restaurants. Then we would spend evenings and mornings playing Mah Jongg. When my friend sold her timeshare and bought a house in Monticello, New York, we still loved Shawnee so much that we now expanded our trips to twice a year, one weekend in Pennsylvania where we rented a house, and one in Monticello. Recently we decided to try a place in New Hope instead of Shawnee. We had a great time there also.

We developed a loose routine. Those who wanted to shop went shopping, those who wanted to go to the casino went there, those who wanted to stay in the house stayed. We always had several cars going in diverse directions. One of the activities that some of the women loved was antiquing, and they found places to pursue that activity. I was never a big fan of antiquing and I only went if everyone was going somewhere together afterward. There was one shop in the Monticello area that I didn't mind going to. It was neater and better organized than most of the other shops.

We stopped there one day on the way to somewhere else. The shop had several small rooms. My friend was looking at something in a showcase of jewelry in one of the rooms. As I gazed across the showcase, something caught my eye. It was a watch with a pretty, unusual band and a pearlized face. It contained stones that were either rhinestones or CZs. I am always on the lookout for unusual jewelry and this really caught my attention. I kind of dismissed it, figuring that it was probably priced higher than anything I wanted to buy as just a spur of the moment thing that I did not really need. "Look at the price," my friend exclaimed. She had spotted the price tag. My mouth dropped open as I saw the price tag of $15!!

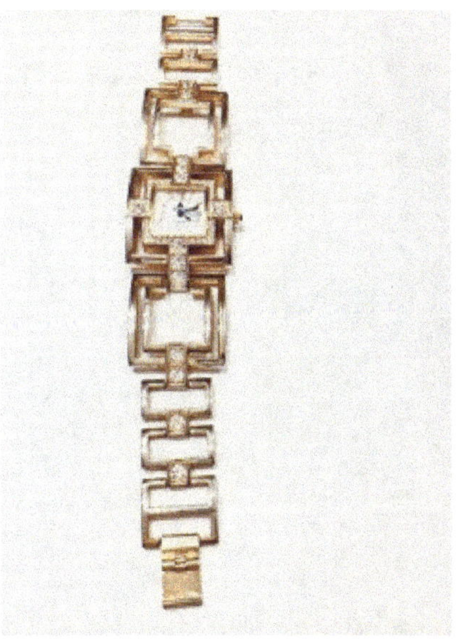

"Well," I answered. "It's probably broken and unfixable."

"Ask the lady," she persisted. So I brought the proprietor over and she assured me that it only needed a battery. I figured even if she was wrong, all I would lose was $15 so I took it. I have accumulated more than a few watches over my lifetime. Some have gone out of style, some have broken, but I still have about a half dozen that I wear. This $15 watch has become one of my favorites. It is just my style, and I get compliments on it all the time. It is even dressy enough to wear on special occasions. My son noticed it at a party and remarked on my attractive new watch. It makes me laugh. It is one of my best bargains and always a reminder of the wonderful weekends with my friends.

Contributed by Janet Metz Walter

THE DIAMOND SCAM

I was in Cape Town South Africa in a restaurant. I spotted a rather large diamond under the table. I picked it up and asked the manager if anyone had reported a missing stone. He said that someone had reported a missing engagement ring.

I told him that I had only found a stone. He asked me for it, but I would not give it to him since no one had reported losing a stone. I went back and looked around to see if I saw a ring anywhere, but I did not.

He was a little annoyed, but I'm a tough cookie and stood my ground. I wasn't trying to steal anything, but I did not trust him either.

I gave him my contact information and told him that I would give the stone back to whoever reported it missing and could identify it.

When I got home, I decided to take it into a local jewelry store to determine the value of the stone.

I found out that the stone was a very good fake diamond. These diamonds are displayed in shop windows as real stones. When people come in to buy jewelry, they pick out and pay for a diamond; then when the jeweler goes to set it into the ring or other piece of jewelry, he switches the real diamond for one of these fabulous fakes. I surmised that someone who was carrying or selling these stones had eaten in the restaurant and dropped one of the stones. I keep it as a memento of my trip.

Contributed by Lucille Siegel

TOLEDO DAMASCENE

There is a city in Spain called Toledo. It is famous for a certain style of jewelry called Damascene. It was known for centuries in ancient Egypt, Greece, Rome, and other civilizations. Around the 15th Century, it became popular in Europe; and Toledo became the center of manufacture of this jewelry.

The jewelry is crafted by inlaying different metals, usually gold and silver, in intricate patterns of flower and bird motifs, and sometimes geometrics. The metals are inlaid into a darkly oxidized steel or other black background. It is very unique looking. It has been said that it is now a tourist industry and that Spanish women do not wear this jewelry.

When I was in Toledo in the early 70's I bought a bracelet for myself and one for my mother. I was disappointed when mine broke; but when my mother passed away, I inherited hers which was a different design. But I always enjoyed wearing it.

In 2017 I went back to Spain for the first time and was determined to find some more Damascene jewelry. Of course, much of it is now mass produced, but I still love the look.

Touring in Barcelona was awesome. It quickly became one of my favorite European cities. Much of the architecture there was designed by Antoni Gaudi, who is famous for using mosaics, ceramic tile, and patterned brick and stone in a combination of various architectural styles to create different colorful and unusual structures. In many of these structures, his designs are derived from themes in nature. His most famous work is the magnificent Sagrada Familia cathedral which he started working on in 1883, and to this day parts of it are still being built.

Eventually, I found a shop in Barcelona that carried the Damascene jewelry. I was sure it was mass-produced, as there was a whole wall of it hanging on cards in the store, but I did not care. If this was what was available, this was what I was buying, especially since I was not in Toledo, so I bought an earring and pendant set.

When I was in a different store, I found a ring that I fell in love with.

Whether it is mass-produced or not it is still a unique process and design associated with Spain, and I always get compliments when I wear it.

Contributed by Janet Metz Walter

THE ELEPHANT HAIR RING

I was born in Brussels, Belgium. My family moved around a lot; and eventually, we wound up in a municipality called Silly. That was really the name!

It was a simple place, and jewelry was not a big part of my life. I really had no interest in it.

I met my husband on an extended vacation traveling throughout the United States. We fell in love in a very short time. He then came to Belgium to propose, and we were married in Silly in 1984. After the wedding, he brought me back to California.

We moved into a fairly modest house that had a large back yard with a swimming pool and a deck. I love to garden, and I turned the back yard and the deck into a large garden that I tend to every day.

In 1987 we took a safari to Kenya. Africans revere elephants, and for 1500 years they have made jewelry out of elephant hair that used to get caught on the thorn trees from their tails. They developed certain designs; and they believed that the jewelry brought people good luck, and good health, love, and happiness.

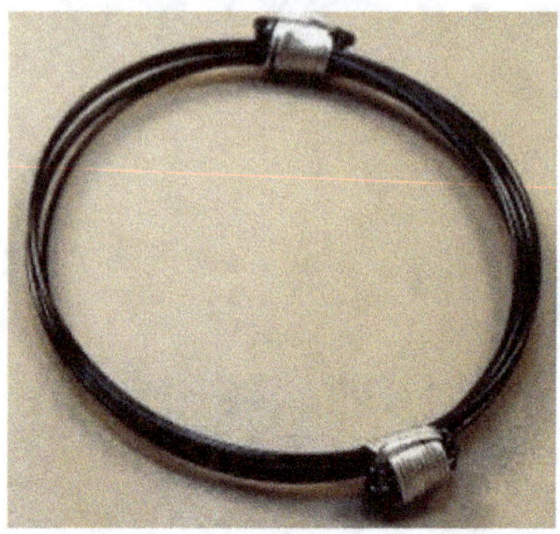

My husband wanted to buy us both gifts. By that time some of the elephant hair jewelry was made from poached elephants; and when poaching became illegal, they started making the jewelry out of precious metals to resemble the elephant hair jewelry.

My husband found a real elephant hair bracelet for himself but bought me a gold ring that was a copy of an elephant hair ring.

I loved that ring because it was beautiful and adjustable to my fingers when they became a little swollen.

One day I was planting in my garden, and the ring fell off my finger. When I realized it was gone, I dug all around the bed I was working in but could not find it. I was very upset to have lost it because it was one of the few pieces of jewelry that I wore and loved.

Almost two years later I was putting some new tulip bulbs in the garden; and as I was digging and turning over the dirt, the ring suddenly appeared. It was a miracle. It had been in the flower bed all that time. It was amazing that it had not gotten displaced by rain or my digging in the bed.

I was so happy and lucky to have found it and was able to wear my favorite piece of jewelry again.

Contributed by Pascale

EARRING STORIES

My husband, Mark, and I do a lot of traveling; and we collect souvenirs and/or jewelry wherever we go.

On one occasion, we were traveling to Italy. I wanted to buy a pair of cameo earrings, as Italy is known for cameo jewelry.

The tour guide told us that we were going to the factory at the end of the tour and that we should wait until then to buy our jewelry, as the factory gave certificates of authenticity and street vendors and small stores did not.

We had a lovely tour of Rome and Venice.

On the day we were supposed to go to the factory, I was so excited that I would be able to shop and find my earrings. Then the tour guide gave us the bad news. The factory was closed due to a strike. It was the last day of the tour. I was sorry that I hadn't at least bought something somewhere along the way. It was a good lesson.

I bid *Arrivederci* to Rome, the Leaning Tower of Pisa, Saint Mark's Square in Venice, and to my cameo earrings.

Sometime later, still yearning for cameo jewelry, I bought a cameo ring in a local store and then bought the matching earrings. I took a trip to Buffalo; and when I got to my hotel room after dinner, I realized that I was missing an earring. I was sure it was gone for good, but we decided to go back down to the dining room of the hotel to look for it. Sure enough, we found it on the floor of the dining room. I was very happy to have found them, but that would not be the last time that I lost earrings.

In 2013 we were on a cruise to Burma (Myanmar.) It was New Year's Eve and there was a show of cultural dancing and a lot of celebrating on the beach. I was wearing a pair of Sterling Silver and Orange drop earrings. They had been a gift from a friend.

I suddenly noticed that I was missing an earring. I realized there was little hope of finding it, but a waiter who knew I was upset gathered together all the other waiters. "We will find it" they declared. They combed the sand in the area where we were; and sure enough, someone found the earring!

Happy New Year To Me!

Contributed by Janet Levine

THE BIGGEST BARGAIN IN THE WORLD

To some people the best vacation is going to a sunny island in the Caribbean, parking yourself in a hotel and relaxing on the beach with drinks, snacks and suntan lotion. It could also include an occasional outing into town to dine or shop.

To others, cruising around to a few islands provides a great combination of diverse surroundings, relaxing on the beach or on the boat and maybe a little sightseeing excursion thrown in.

But let's not forget the shopping! Many port towns have shopping villages or a main shopping street, where you can find bargains on designer clothing, accessories and jewelry. If you have been to the port enough times you know where you like to shop.

A few years ago we sailed into Puerto Rico on a cruise and passengers scattered through the town to hunt for bargains.

I was wandering around a souvenir shop that sold T shirts, hats, mugs and other typical memorabilia of the area. In one locked glass cabinet that displayed costume jewelry, I spotted a bracelet that appealed to me. It looked like a diamond bracelet, but I did not believe that this shop would be carrying diamond bracelets, so I asked how much it was.

"Two hundred and fifty dollars" was the surprising reply. It seemed slightly expensive for that kind of shop, and I bargained him down to two hundred dollars.

The problem was that the bracelet was a little too large for my wrist and I needed some links taken out. I put it away in my suitcase with the intention of having the links taken out when I got home.

When the vacation was over I took the bracelet to my local jeweler to remove the links.

"How much do you charge to remove the links?" I asked him, expecting to hear something like twenty dollars.

"A hundred and fifty dollars" was his shocking reply.

"What?" I asked a little taken aback. "I only paid two hundred dollars for the bracelet. How can you charge a hundred and fifty to take out a few links?"

"Well this is a diamond bracelet" he replied, a little indignant. "That's how much I charge for removing the links."

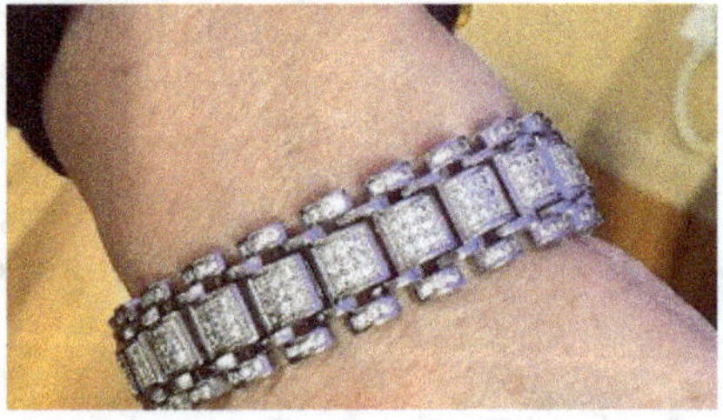

"It's a diamond bracelet?" I repeated, confused. "Are you sure?" He must have thought I was a little strange.

"Yes I am sure," he assured me. After chewing on this tidbit of information for a minute, I addressed him again.

"Can you give me an estimate of how much it is worth?" I asked him, anxiously awaiting the answer.

He looked it over again and told me that he would appraise it at $11,500. You could have knocked me over with one finger. He offered me $7000 cash if I wanted to sell him the bracelet.

Now I had a choice. I could make a lot of money selling the bracelet, but I decided that I bought it because I liked it and I was going to keep it and enjoy it. I paid him the $150 to take out the links, and I do greatly enjoy wearing it. It was the bargain of a lifetime.

Contributed by Robin H

ACKNOWLEDGMENTS

I met Stephanie Sands Larkin at a networking meeting. She announced that she was holding a workshop for first time authors and I decided to attend. Stephanie explained that not every book has to be a major work. People who have businesses can write a book relating to the business, and what's more, you can use contributions from other people to make the book interesting and informative. Something rang in my head and I suddenly realized that I could make a lifelong dream come true.

I met with Stephanie the Publisher, who went on to become Stephanie my Mah Jongg student, who went on to become Stephanie my friend!

Thank you for your guidance, your patience, your never-ending good humor and your time and effort which you always seemed to find even at 1AM or on vacation, or in between a million other things you were doing. You made my dream come true!

What would this book be without all of the enthusiastic people who came forward with stories for me? From my dearest friends, to people I grew up with. From friends of friends, relatives of friends, and professional friends, I have made a whole slew of new friends and this book never could have been written without you.

I add to that my grandson, and friends Ellen B and Karen C who spent hours with me checking the edited versions of the stories to make sure they were accurate and ready to submit to the publisher; and to all the friends and family who may not have been directly involved with the book but have been so excited and supportive.

Thank you from the bottom of my heart.

Of course I have to thank my party and travel loving husband Ken for his sense of humor, hard work and unending devotion to his family, who constantly supplied me with jewelry, and taught me all about the business. His love of travel has taken me all over the world, to places I never dreamed of seeing, and adventures I never expected to have, much less finding such interesting jewelry for my collection, and maybe enough adventure stories for the next book!

I could not do without the help and support of my daughter, Donna, Real Estate Agent by trade and the best party and family activity planner who always finds fabulous activities to enjoy wherever we are, and my son and daughter-in-law who always welcome us for a visit and even after 19 years of visits always find new things to do and places to dine. You all have made great efforts to make us a beautiful, fun, and loving family. You all caught the travel bug early and were and still are the best travelers ever!

Last but by no means least, I need to thank my biggest supporters—my three grandchildren, all avid readers with many other talents who are beside themselves with excitement that Grandma wrote a book!

You have been my cheerleaders from the start and I love you with all my heart!

ABOUT THE AUTHOR

Janet Metz Walter grew up in Queens New York. She attended Hunter College in NYC and graduated with a Bachelor of Science Degree in Home Economics, and a minor in Sociology. She realized very early in life that she wanted to write at the very least as an avocation.

After graduation she was employed as a Home Economist for the NYC Dept. of Social Service working with case workers, clients, and in a senior center until her son was born.

Her husband Ken got a job with a fine jewelry company and eventually went into his own business, Gold Fire Diamonds, as a wholesaler and manufacturer of diamond jewelry.

After her son and daughter started school, Janet held jobs in a private social services agency, and a nutrition related PR firm. She then worked as Assistant Director and Food Service Manager of a large child care center.Throughout her career she was involved in writing local newsletters and professional articles. She also became a part time Travel Agent.

This led to the family becoming world travelers. Although her husband was in the jewelry business, Janet developed an interest in the locally crafted jewelry of the places that she explored.

When Janet left her last job, her husband was in the process of moving his business into the world of e commerce. She joined him in the business becoming the curator of the website, and helping with PR and Marketing. Janet also has a second career teaching the game of Mah Jongg in Adult Continuing Education, and privately.

Her love of music and theater helped her to become involved in music and drama programs in camps, in a school age program and in a community theater group where she spent twelve years writing, producing and helping to direct their productions.

Although they still do some wholesale business, Gold Fire Diamonds specializes in personalized service to clients, helping them buy or design jewelry to fit their taste and budget, or repurpose old or inherited jewelry into pieces that they can enjoy and still treasure.

Contact us at info@goldfirediamonds.com for more information.